Hath the Rain a Father?

Hath the Rain a Father? *by* Juanita Casey

ILLUSTRATED *by* THE AUTHOR

Phoenix House
London

Set by the Aldine Press · Letchworth · Herts
and printed by
Latimer Trend & Co. Ltd · Whitstable · Kent
for J. M. DENT & SONS LTD
Aldine House · Bedford Street · London

A Phoenix House publication

First published 1966

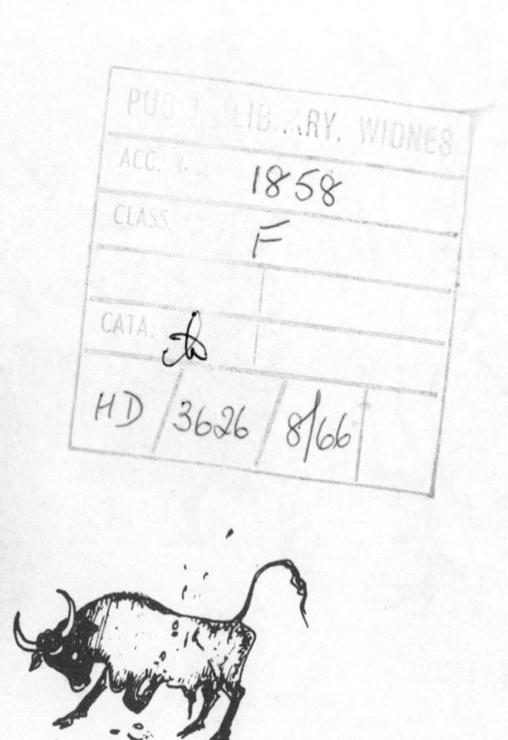

Contents

Stories:

We and our bitterness have left no traces
On Munster grass and Connemara skies.

YEATS

Gold & Silver

I had a little silver hen
And snow-white eggs she'd lay
Which shone like little silver moons
Within her nest of hay.

I had a little cock of gold
Who shone just like the sun
He clapped his wings and sang with joy
To greet the welcome dawn.

And now I have a little flock
Of silver birds, and gold,
Who shine as though the sun and moon
Had flown down to their fold.

'. . . Hath the rain a father? or who hath begotten the drops of dew?
'Hast thou given the horse strength?' . . .

THE BOOK OF JOB

Hath the Rain a Father?

A TRAVELLING man, he was; a travelling man, Roman same as us, they said. Only his heart was broke.

There was some trouble down the road that night you was born and the poor dear man mazed with it all. We had her up by us and our Len run his legs off to get the doctor, but she didn't want anything: she was that quiet, no chavvy, nothing, no rousing her at all.

You couldn't tell she'd gone, she was that quiet.

And then the great star fell down on us like nothing we seen before or since; Benny said it was for a sign. No, nothing like it before or since.

We helped your Dad best we could, but he said he'd go on. He took the small horse and left soon as he'd buried her, and left us the big old mare with the blondy mane, she had her foal the selfsame night as you was born.

Both dropped together the same hour. He left her go and said he'd call again but he never come. He never came back at all.

And we was glad there was no one with a bebby along of us then, only yer Uncle Benny's maid used to stop with us from Sussex way, and she was rearing her one on the artificial.

So we give yer old Blondie's milk, cause there weren't a cow then within miles of this place. Ar, good old mare she were, had a number of nice little horses from her. Best was from that black trotting horse your Uncle Jesse had awhile.

Gor—couldn't he go! Cause he's not your Uncle Jesse in a manner o' speaking, being no relation like in blood, but we'm all your uncles and aunties, my Dosha.

And I can remember the mare Blondie because she meant a great deal to me, it was secret how much she meant to me, even to Auntie Priss whom I loved. Summer sunlight was Blondie's mane when it was caught by the wind like the moving of cornfields, or winter sunlight when the long edges of her coat and the hairs under her jaws became orange, as though she was alight and smoking in the coming frost in the night. To lie and watch her taking shape in the dawn light as if she wasn't just our Blondie, but had begun ten thousand years before and was still here, and would go on being Horse for ever. That was day's beginning, and she would turn into day and become just a horse, big in the belly and well known, smelling sweet and not secret any more. Just Blondie, a chestnut mare with a long pale mane like old rope and big battered horny feet. You might move on in the wagon or walk a turn beside her and pull her blind head in the blinkers unresisting towards you, and there would be her eye, calm, shining out from behind the dark leather, obedient, yet still Horse, still secret Horse: herself. And at the stopping place I'd help unharness her, except her collar which was too heavy, and I couldn't manage the stiff buckles of her girth, pulling at her heavy tail, the only part of her that ever resisted, trying to pull the crupper from where she clamped tail to rump.

She was hard like rubber under the tail, yet soft as velvet where the dock ran down into a point underneath the matted hair, the same sort of point you can find on some old silver spoons. I'd pull her bridle over her wet ears and there was her eye, still obedient, though more Horse. Her bit would fall out of her teeth with a hollow clonk, and rubbing her lips together she'd move away to graze. Sometimes she'd stop after a minute, and making preparations by getting her feet as firm as she could, because she was old, she would shake herself with a shrubbery sound, grunting.

She never got down and rolled because she had a big belly and was old and stiff, so she liked to have her back rubbed for her,

rocking backwards and forwards with pleasure while my hands dug into her greasy hair like forks, with her eyes gone stupid and her lower lip flapping like the clapper on a bell.

The light would go and Blondie would melt into the dusk into her secret ageless darkness, so big you couldn't tell the edges of dusk of where horse began, was or ended.

Night time was all horse; the mare, a black heavy earth-cloud, moving over the grass like the clouds grazing the moon's grass.

Some nights the crescent of her white face drifted like a small new moon, a new horse moon, but not to follow a road like the sky's moon, but to ghost along low over the dew, or to hang motionless half way between sky and grass while she dozed standing. Or to be flung quivering among the trees where she saw something strange to trouble her night. Then her head carved its dark rocks out from the bed of the sky and her eye flashed cold like a star and then gone. And I would be asleep with the eyes of stars and the mare of the night and the night's mind of the mare in my head.

As I grew and she became older and the hairs round her dangling lips turned grey, still she didn't become any less in my eyes. She was still great in the barrel and big-hipped like a big woman, but more than a woman and simpler, being a horse, and as little Carrie, Uncle Benny's 'baby', had gone with her mother back to her Da's home, I was left alone with none else to play with but the old toys Uncle Benny brought back with him from his ragging or calling, the company of my very own longtail pup, the fierce little cock and his six hens, and the black hen who vanished in the spring to brood her ten eggs in the holly bushes, before reappearing with a string of black chicks as proud as a little lady with a string of pearls.

Every year my Auntie Priss said she'd gone by the fox for sure, and Uncle Benny said no, don't be daft, you always says that year in, year out and every time she'll confound you, and every year she sat and I bid quiet even if I did know where she was, quiet as a little saint in the hollies, with her thoughts turned into herself and her quickness all slowed down, waiting for tappings and peepings that opened up her whole world into a miracle for her, of the hard white eggs opened and useless to be thrown out of the way and the black complaining morsels to be warmed and dried by her love into soft chicks, her own little chavvies, for whom she'd die for love.

And then the gathering, the cluckings, the hesitations, the first few steps, the waits, the cautions, the protections of hen-mother, body swelled with fierce love, and the final entrance into the world beyond the bushes, over the open grass space to our huts, dipping and sailing like a blown leaf, ready to fly into the mare's face or hurl at the dog's, and Auntie Priss laughing and Gran fussing like a hen herself to get a little corn, and the red cock running to see his new family, escorting them to the corn, picking up a grain and calling them to him, stepping back like a little gentleman so that they might be sure to see it. It made us all happy to see them, for the time of year when chicks come out is a good time, and made more to our family, them and my growing pup who would one day be fast enough to run into the downland hares, and the mare, whom I watched and loved and knew better than anyone, even a mother.

I never forgot it was her milk that raised me and her own colt together, and that made the colt my brother, and all the nation of horses.

And then came the bad winter and Blondie became ill. She stood about with her back to the wind not eating, and although we did as much as lay in our power to help her with good hay, going short to give her corn, Auntie Priss said at length she couldn't bear to see the poor old horse go down and why didn't Benny get the vet and end it, and Uncle Benny said if she was still failing the next day he'd get the man along from the kennels. And I took her poor bony head in my arms and tried to shut her dull eyes and said please Blondie die before tomorrow. Don't let them shoot you and give you to all the dogs. Fall down and die peaceful, Blondie, or else please God make you better.

But I knew she was finished, she was just a flicker in a frame of bones, the skin dead already. Yet when I saw her swollen shape in the first light next morning and the big yellow teeth with the hay still clenched between them, and her poor unseeing eye, the complete collapse as though the finest palace has fallen which is a dead horse, I wept bitterly and flung myself down against her neck until Uncle Benny gently picked me up and carried me to Gran for comfort. O my Mum, I cried unknowingly, O my Mum, my Mum.

There was no burial for Blondie like there was when old Gran Cooper died. Uncle Benny got the man from the kennels in his lorry and they fastened a chain round her neck and dragged her stiff and resisting over the ground and up into the lorry. The grass was all flat like a path after her, where her great bony shoulders and hips scored up the ground, and her mouth fell open over the bumps.

One hind leg got caught up on the lorry and they cursed and pushed it. At last the lorry pulled away, but the sacks fell off with the jolting, leaving the leg stiffly waving over the side.

If only she could have lasted another two weeks then the spring grass would have been through, but she had to go. It was as if her battle with winter could be won only the one way, although the skies were blue and warm, and the promise was there, to have balanced on and recovered for the summer only to fall at the first frost, would have been to no purpose. Her life ran its course, and then ran down and ended. To have gone on, even a minute over her time, would have been no part of the plan that was her morality, her edifice, her ordination.

Then we moved on, spring was come, the winter camp and Blondie left behind for another year, and in the noise and excitement, shouts and orders, the keen edge of her death blunted a little in my mind, and I was given her three-year-old colt Ranter to teach him manners and get him used to the road. Soon he'd be harnessed beside Mary, the Welsh mare who pulled our biggest van, Gran's van. It was a small van as some go, not all twiddly bits and brass like the beauties some of the Herons had, but Mary was getting on and needed help on the hills, and Ranter would be fastened in beside her and left to her. She would teach him to pull quicker than anything we could do. Meanwhile I had charge of him, to get him used to the traffic before he breasted his first collar.

Different nights we pulled into different places, some lonely, some unexpected, when we met up with relations or other travelling families and bided a while with them. There'd be peg-making and calling for us all, work on the farms around and playing and fighting for all us chavvies. And trading. Uncle Benny chopped my Ranter for a little bitty pony who had been in a circus and was pleased at the deal, for the pony was spotted like a plum-pudding dog, and Uncle Benny had always wanted a spotted horse.

But I was angry, and sauced Uncle Benny for having the wrong side of the bargain, until I got my head cuffed, for Ranter was a fine-stepping young cob with a good heart, and the spot was small and mean and had pale blue eyes like a red-headed woman, and was an entire besides, always squealing off at the mares.

But he drew the people's gaze when we went into the towns, and that was a good thing, and made them buy. Gran sat stiff as a queen and sold her flowers to the people, and I used to watch them because it was more than just selling flowers to them, it was as though she was a mother of the earth, like that old goddess, and as though she was handing over wisdom to the people with the flowers. Yellow flowers of the sun, and lovely daffs, lady, only a sixpence. Only a sixpence for the key that opens the eye of the sun, and that which lies in the heart to be opened by the sun, the lover, the loved one of earth's body.

Golden, like the thrones of old kings and like the shining water-suns, the golden eyes of the big mother toads in springtime.

Blue flowers, lady, of the blue road we know as well as the grain of our hand. Long blue road under a wet sky and a cold wind, every dip and rise we know, the patch of centaury in summer by the ditch with the grating, the hollow under the thorn hedge to slip into in winter when the basket is heavy. The cold wind, lady, which fingers the cold face and says it will be like this when death comes. Blue flowers. A bunch of life, lady, or a little posy of death. And they look into Gran's eyes; hopeful, frightened and suspicious, the brazen, the weak, the hopeless, the fools, the ones with good hearts and the many with bad.

For comfort, for some magical contact, for curiosity, they look for a moment into Gran's alien eyes and go away with their flowers.

And when we'd made enough to get our tea and a bit of ham and as much as we could besides, then Gran would drive out of town like a queen in a chariot with a spatter of hooves and the spotted pony with the jackdaw eyes going like a bomb.

Past the Travellers Rest, with the notice which said No Gypsies Here, which Gran couldn't read although she said she knew by the shape on it, to the Greyhound where Gran would go in all nods and smiles while I waited with the spot. Shan't be long, child, corse you knows very well I can't take it like I used. At closing time she'd get up into the cart as nimble as a ferret, but I'd have to drive the spot as she kept falling to one side or the other asleep—finally I would settle her down on the floor and put the spot at the last hill at a gallop, all the chains ringing like a church and the harness bouncing almost off his back altogether.

Auntie Priss was cross with me, and Uncle Benny outraged as usual, but we told him he's a fine one to talk and helped Gran into the tent and left her to sleep.

Some days after we crossed the borders of Dorset, at least where it's said to be, although to us the road is the same, the hedges green the same, and the sun comes up no different because we've crossed a boundary. We pulled up a steep hill and up into a chalky lane to the beginning of the downs. There had been other travellers before us as we could see by the marks of the wheels and horses, and we made our bit of fire on the black spot where theirs had been. I went to get wood among the big beeches down the hill, and right across the valley, in the evening air, there was a ribbon of smoke rising straight as a willow from a field down the end of a lane. That's a traveller's fire, said my Uncle Benny, or else I'm my Uncle Noah's jack-donkey. Funny how's you can tell. Wonder who 'tis? There's Lees these parts, or it might be old Tianni Draper and her lot. When we got back supper was doing and Uncle Benny decided to take the cart next morning and go searching. Searching meant anything; from old anvils to chicken houses, a load of sentimental oil prints in gilt frames, a few old chairs, some soup tureens, a clutch of pheasants' eggs from the woods, or a gramophone with a pile of old records which he would bring home delighted; and then, as none of us could read, we'd have to wait until the music played to tell what they were.

Beethoven was taken off long before the end, but a sorrowful tenor and the 'Rose of Tralee' brought tears and exclamations.

The suspense was awful. The gramophone had to be held down with one hand and cranked up with the other, and as there weren't any needles as a rule Uncle Benny would cut a thorn and fit that in; and if we were talking he'd shout Order now, Order, as though someone was going to sing in the public-house, and then the thorn was dropped and we would all watch as though hypnotized the whirling black round as it hissed and crackled for a few rings until the music came, and when it did we all felt unbearably relieved.

The relief was so great to Gran after the long preparations and the anxiety of waiting for the first sound, she used to say it had the same effect on her spirit as castor oil.

Next day it rained, and we never did find out which travellers they were, stopping over in the valley. Perhaps they stayed on that day because of the rain or maybe they struggled like us with damp harness and wet horses, the time when your fingers slip and you hit hard on the shaft enough to cry.

I never liked rain; you got used to it in your boots if they had a hole, but it dulled the brass on the harness and you had no pride in it left.

Christmas we always had pork. Most travellers do, as they like a bit of pork. And a good suet pudding. Christmas was always full of sharp butchers' holly which poisoned you if you weren't careful of the pricks, and we made flowers out of wax and stuck them on to the points and sold them in little pots with moss.

Potted plants are dear for householders to buy in winter.

Ferns too we used to get, and the older ones would make chrysanthemum heads from shaving sticks down cleverly, but not many of the young ones can make them. Crab-apples painted and stuck on to silvered branches look nice too. It's surprising what you can do. We used to try and give the horses a bit extra over Christmas too, and the dogs were always bloated, just this once.

One place in Hampshire we used to stop over Christmas because of the good supply of holly and crab-apples you got there, and we used to call at the big houses, and a lot of building was going on. There was an old white horse that had carried a policeman buried near by; he was full of bits of iron from the first war which used to come out of him right up to the day he died. He died at over thirty, and they put up a stone for him and built a golf-course round him. Shameful waste of good grass, Uncle Benny used to say. There was a big garden which they were going to build on, and it had a lake in it and a huge tree which you couldn't climb up far because it was so thick, with dropped twigs and made its own thatch. It was a kind of pine and used to grow clumps of yellow toadstools underneath it, all pushing up under the pine needles.

The people had a grave for a dog in the kitchen garden, near some violets growing, and a big stone surrounded by iron rails, where two carriage-horses had been buried years and years ago. The last Christmas we spent there they had built all over the lawns and only one old beech tree was left, where we used to play over its long snaky roots, trying not to fall off into 'the sea'.

We couldn't go there again, and the blacksmith closed too. They made a knitting shop there and painted it blue.

It was funny how mostly you disremembered the rain and how it was always sunny. You seemed to be under green leaves all the time when you thought back, and fields with buttercups and big white ox-daisies and butterfat ponies in them. Sometimes we put ours in with them at night and got them out in the first light, leaving long trails through the dew like rabbits.

And then I grew breasts and none of my things fitted me, there was either old holey coats off old ladies, too big, or everything too small. I couldn't take the knocks playing as I used, and when I got up on a horse I started to see the men watching my knees, as you can't grip a horse without your skirt round your waist sometimes. It was fun and a bit dangerous, Men and Horses. And your knees grew eyes back. Then Jimmy King kissed me one day at the back of the Conservative Club, the night they hit poor Uncle Benny with a bottle in mistake for someone else and we fell over him in the struggle, but I was too busy to mind him, with my hands full as you might say. And Amy's old man who got a corset off someone, and danced on a table till it broke. And another man, a sailor, who burned himself with newspaper and singed all his chest hair off, which he hadn't meant to. That was a night. Christmas Eve. Kelly chopped his wife for one of the Smiths and got an old pram and ten shillings with her and wheeled her home, and Henry Long beat his with an axe and burned down his tent while his wife chopped up all the harness and smashed the plates, which they did every Christmas, ever since we knew them.

And then I grew up altogether.

The Sacrifice

NOT so very long ago there was an old man whose name was Magilligan. He lived on the side of a mountain in a small white cabin which huddled under its thatch against the weather, and he kept the thatch secure with heavy stones. The cabin had one door and three windows—two in front and one at the back. The front windows looked out upon a small brown potato patch, then a battered green gate, and beyond the gate away to the great lake and the mountains. The back window looked out upon a small thatched shed where lived Magilligan's pig, an old white nanny-goat and his ten black hens. A fine-eyed brown dog and a linnet in a home-made cage shared the cabin with Magilligan, and a low white wall enclosed them all and kept out the mountain.

The she-goat went out every morning to forage, and returned at dusk to her master to be milked and to spend her nights with the warm black pigs and the black hens.

Now Magilligan also had a he-goat, but he was not of the regular household; he lived out on the mountain, only coming down to the cabin in severe weather, when he would jump the low wall and make life unbearable for the nanny-goat, the motherly pig and the hens, with his overbearing manners and the pungency of his smell. At dawn he would be away up the mountain again, leaving only the smell behind to let Magilligan know of his visit.

Once a year, at blackberry time, an urge would come upon the she-goat, and she would trot forth to climb the mountain with jiggling tail and plaintive bleat, and her day would be spent

dancing, fencing and mating.

Then she would leave her heavy-horned lover and return down the winding track to her master's home. Old Magilligan would greet her kindly, and she would tell him of her day, for they had a great understanding between them.

And high up on the mountain, where the moon crept fox-like over its shoulder, lay the he-goat, his black knees cupped to the hard short grasses, his horns flaring like the wide wings of a wicked angel. The moon's light lay as cold and as old as in the beginning of things, and the same understanding burned in the yellow eye of the he-goat. Goat and moon knew each other well.

Now very few people had seen Magilligan's goat; he rarely came down from the mountain, and the times he had they very properly crossed themselves and hurried past.

None had ever stopped to pass the time of day, and none had disputed the right of way if he was upon the road.

This was good, and as it should be to the he-goat, who considered the gentle Magilligan, his house and his possessions all came within the kingdom that the he-goat considered his alone to rule.

One thing only he wished for, and that was when, lonely sometimes on his mountain, by night or by day, he craved companionship.

He desired that people would stand around him once in a while and sing and talk to him and make pleasant music to enchant his ears, for it would appear useless to stand alone, the ruler of a kingdom, without someone to tell him it was so now and again.

It was both lonely and thankless to be always in such an exalted position, even though he ruled a whole mountain and was regarded by Magilligan with deep respect and a very proper awe.

Now one fine warm day, in a small town some seven miles from the mountain, there was held a great fair, and to it every year came hundreds of people, walking, on horseback, by jaunting car and wagon. Farmers, tinkers, priests and pedlars all poured into the little town to buy and sell, pray and steal, drink and sing until it nearly burst itself with the noise.

Scores of horses were run up and down through the streets and everyone went in peril of their lives from the flying hooves, but as they were all Irishmen nobody minded at all, and the enjoyment was enormous all round.

During the three days of Old Harry that the fair brought to the little town, it had been the custom for as long as people could remember to include a he-goat in the celebrations.

The priests might smile in kindly tolerance, and the little girls in white might laugh and dance, but there were some who knew of other, deeper things with an ancient hidden knowledge. . . .

So many people were upon the little road which wound past Magilligan's cabin that day that the black he-goat came stepping sharply down from the mountain to see what was about, but as he reached the battered green gate out came Magilligan with many praises for his timely appearance, and before he realized it there was a rope over his neck and around his horns, his feet were lashed together and he was lying on the ground trussed as surely as might be one of the ten black hens.

He was not one to fight against misfortune, but kept a silent dignity as he was pushed and hoisted on to a cart and driven off by a stranger down the road away from the mountain.

Only his eyes moved, like slit suns.

A shackled goat-god, he would await his time—but it would be very sure.

The noise as they entered the little town beat upon his ears like the roar of a crazy sea, but though all was strange around him the he-goat felt no fear, only a great fever began to shake in his heart, that now stirred with an old forgotten knowledge, old as the goat-eyed moon. Then men came and took away his ropes; he was driven around the town, standing uncomfortably in a mess of greenery at the feet of a small girl who was a queen for the day, as he should be king.

Between his flaring horns the child placed a golden crown, and he was lifted high above the crowd. He stared down upon them, a crowned horned god, and they shouted and sang to him, and the little girls in white laughed and danced beneath him. The he-goat grinned.

He was their god; to whom they must, at last, give homage, from whom he must demand his sacrifice. Something written on a page of time by a devil's hand, something that had to be fulfilled from far down in the dark caves of man's brain, goat's brain, something long remembered, long awaited. That is what men say.

It came when his cage was at last lowered and opened. He flamed out arrow-straight, rocketed from hell, a horned vengeance.

This was his right; now he fulfilled a forgotten destiny. His neck was heavy with intent and in his eye shone chaos. That is what men say.

There was a silence now over the little town where the child in white lay; she had worn a golden crown too, and had placed the other with touching ceremony, a little fearful, upon the black goat's head, a frail sacrifice to a goat-god, who had this moment avenged the now forgotten centuries when men destroyed the proudest of his horned race for the glory of their own gods. That is what men say. And then the he-goat flung out upon the road and ran high and light to the mountain. As he climbed, the great light died from his eye; his knees at last bent to the well-worn hollow among the rocks, and he watched for a time the tiny winking light far below that was Magilligan's cabin window.

All was quiet in his heart; knowing of neither good nor evil, how could either trouble goat, though they be man's despair? The moon stole along her vixen's track over the mountain and her light shone coldly on the little white cabin with its one yellow eye still open, shivered on the cold-running mountain streams, shimmered wetly on the road a mile below so that it writhed eel-like past the mountain, and stroked the still form of the sleeping he-goat, with his chin turned round to rest upon his back, and a golden crown between his horns.

The Hounds

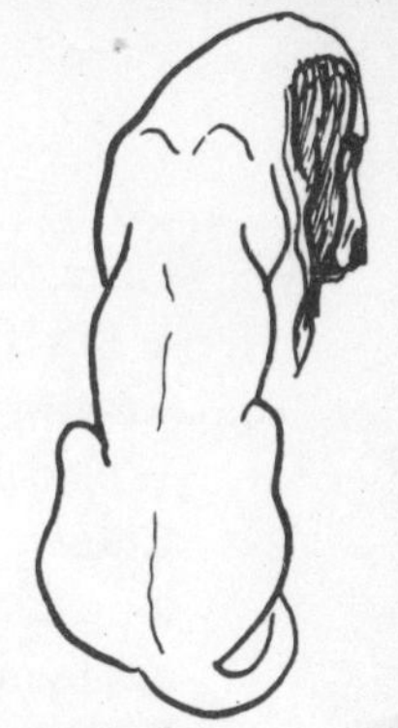

It was Sunday; a week of rain and strong winds had hampered the diggings on the big mound facing the Atlantic.

One man in particular was chafing at the continuous delay due to the weather, and he was a man who as a rule rode down all opposition and over all obstacles as though mounted on the war-horse of his own inexhaustible energy. But weather, Irish weather, had defeated even Henry O. Riordan.

Riordan was not the sort of man most people thought of when you mentioned 'archaeologist': a slight, thin, pedantic professor maybe; not the big bull of a man who now stood beside the great stones of the mound with his collar turned against the thin, persistent, driving rain and his big workman's hands deep in his coat.

Henry Riordan was the most dynamic—and some said the most unsuitable—of any man that had become eminent in this field; his ruthless approach got things done, his energy communicated itself to all his labourers, whether to the dark men of the Nile banks, or the quiet men of Sligo who worked slowly and methodically into the green hillside, but who wondered amongst themselves whether it was right at all to be disturbing who knows what great king—worse, a queen—who had lain so long in the hill. Some of the Egyptians had felt the same; he who gazed on the golden mask of a Pharaoh might fade into the dust himself; there were strange things to be faced if the centuries are turned and lifted as the earth is laid open by a ploughshare . . .

And hadn't Paddy seen the name Oisin on the letter he'd

carried up the hill one day to himself there at the top? 'Henry Oisin Riordan', the letter said, from America, some university.

But Oisin—sure, there's a name now I wouldn't want to be wearing meself. Not at all.

Nor did Henry Riordan; his father's family had come from the County Cork years back; they'd been in Washington, D.C. so long now that it was practically forgotten; only Pa had had the annoying desire to name all the kids with at least one good old Irish name, and old was the word. Could you imagine a sister with Emer (as well as the 'Margaret' his Ma had insisted on) as her middle name, and his other brother George was Parthelon, and he, good grief—Oisin!

To Henry O. Riordan the names of mythology meant nothing; this was strange, as in his calling he had to sift and search in the world of reality, in the earth itself, and to bring out of it things of such antiquity that they belonged to the lost days of the gods and the godlike men.

Often the very name of the place where he worked would be of a mythological giant or hero; but this meant nothing to him; only the reality of a skeleton or a bronze dagger or a shard of pottery interested him; to decipher the shadowy half-world of legend he left to others, for whom he professed a scorn he never bothered to conceal. His attitude caused a great deal of controversy amongst his colleagues, and amongst many of those interested in all aspects of man's spiritual and temporal history; his brilliance of direction and uncanny knowledge of the positions of ancient sites were undoubted; but his refusal to acknowledge the very foundations of man's history in myth or legend was a source of heated argument and comment.

This then was the man who now turned his back on the sea and made his way down the hillside past the black-faced sheep to where his car was parked in a recess of the bending mountain road. The sheep divided in front of him, their tails jerking and their heads high like deer running, much as shoal of fish flash and winnow when a pike is among them. Then, at a distance, they stopped and silently watched him reach the road with only their black noses moving—their yellow eyes unblinking.

Riordan saw their ram watching him; horns curving round his high quick ears, like those which the Egyptians carved from their limestone; the same expression in the eyes, he thought, looking back through the rain. Empty, angry, anxious, challenging, blank? No good putting human emotions to an animal. He slammed the door on the rain; and the ram, shaking his wet ears with a sharp slapping sound, took three steps forward and bent his head again to the short turf between the scattered rocks.

Henry Riordan drove fast, without a glance at the sea to his right, grey and ruffled and with a thick lace of white round the rocks on the beach, which were revealed at each gap where stones had fallen from the old road wall.

Gleninch and the hotel lay at the head of the long reach of water, twelve miles away, with the mountains on one side and the sea on the other. Riordan noticed with satisfaction that far over the water the mountains ahead were showing their crests every now and again as the fast shreds of cloud separated, and the lines of fair weather could be read in the sky's hand much the same as in a man's. A man may frown, and a cloud passes over a mountain, a child laughs and the sun shines; to sleep is but to turn the old moon on to her back. Funny how you remembered things like that; an old man had said it as his child lay dying in a black tent outside Tashkent . . .

The lorries from the big quarry had left a trail of mud as they lurched out on to the road, and this Riordan hit as he cornered in his usual fast swirl. With a feeling of complete disbelief, then as though he were in a no man's land of suspended emotion where he could see everything slowly and plainly but could not bring his mind to believe it, he saw the mountainside leap at him and heard the car scream like an animal; then black, glass and metal, huge sound and pain that are both red, red searching up through orange to white, trembling, blinding, silence.

The sheep, which had startled at the crash and run a short distance up the hillside, turned to watch the torn car with one wheel still turning slowly in the air. It stopped, ran back, then forward; stopped. The sheep relaxed to graze as the small ordinary sounds returned past the silence which transfixes disaster, a trickle of earth followed a falling stone out of the gash in the hill's flank on to the road. The rain hissed in the dead grasses on the wall, and the red line which ran thickly from underneath the car, snaking down the uneven surface of the road, spread a little in the wet, hesitated, fell into a channel with a short rush and vanished into the grass at the roadside . . .

He never knew how he got out; he looked back at the car and the blood which he realized dully must be his own, now mingling with the rain in a sheet of red. No one in sight; nor would there be at this hour of the day in this lonely place. He must get help. He must be hurt, though he dare not look. His head was light and strange; perhaps that was where he was hurt; he felt no pain.

He watched the rain spit on the road ahead but felt no wet, no cold. He could hear and see, thank God, hear a curious belling, insistent sound he couldn't place; it was like the sound made by the wild geese as they fly into the north ways when the spring calls them; like many pigeons in a wood; like the stag's deep bell when he lusts for his hinds; like an organ heard from a distance.

It was like the voices of hounds—why, of course it was, but there were no hounds in these parts, and it was summer. No one hunted in summer. He hadn't realized he was below the great mound: he'd thought he was going the other way, towards Gleninch.

The hounds were nearer now; their voices seemed to come at him from all sides; and then he saw them, slipping in a torrent down the hillside, pouring past the mound more like fish than dogs. He knew enough about animals to know they were in sight of their quarry, though he could see no huntsmen nor what they

were after.

The note now was sustained, deep, purposeful, and their heads were up; they were at sight.

He was not alarmed; he had never feared any animal, but he was at a loss to know what to do if they should come his way; he had never heard of hounds harming anyone, although he would certainly not be fool enough to stand in their way and oppose them if they were near a killing. They were very near now, but he realized suddenly they were silent. He could hear the thuds of breath as they jumped from rock to rock, and then they were all around him on the road.

He put his hand out to the nearest: the animal neither moved away nor came nearer; they all gazed at him panting, but silent, watchful. He saw they were big, smooth hounds, beautifully proportioned, like gazelles. They were a perfectly matched pack; all of them white and all with red ears.

They obviously meant him no harm, but seemed to wait for him to move first.

He turned and they moved behind him; suddenly, unexpectedly, he ran, and their curled tails sprang up and they leaped after him. He stopped.

Their yellow eyes watched him steadily; there was no hate in them, only watchfulness.

They seemed ready to follow him anywhere.

Where had he heard of hounds like these? His head seemed muffled and strange . . . white hounds with red ears . . . O God . . .

'*And the soul of Oisin was pursued by the Hounds of Hell. . . . The white hounds with the red ears pursued the soul of Oisin.*'

Henry Oisin Riordan stood on the road which winds past the mound called Niamh's Isle and looked into the yellow eyes of the hounds around him.

He was aware suddenly that the rain had stopped, and that blue sky was showing between the clouds. Here and there the sun glinted on fields far away, lit up the sea, touched the heather on the mountain. And as suddenly the sun was around the hounds and on himself.

The hounds, dazzlingly white all about him, looked up at him and waited.

And it was then that he saw they cast no shadow among them, and that no shadow lay behind him on the road.

The Sea Beast and the 'Queen of Heaven'

THE porpoises were lazing in the summer sea a fathom deep off the rocks of Barra, idle with content and two pups already in the herd, when the big grey mother rose slowly to the world of air and rested quietly near the pale surface. The small shining body was born into a world of shifting lights and gentle water, a lapping green cradle of water; and he was one with the sea from the moment of his birth. By the side of his wise grey mother the young Barra came to understand the ways of water, and the momentary brightness and strangeness of the world above; of the suddenness of sun's heat by day, and the glittering eyes of night. He learned of the black depths of the sea, and of the great rush of joy when he leaped in a boil of silver into the world of winds, his body curving like the rainbow. He learned how to root out the foolish sole from shallow sands, to hunt the soft-mouthed mullet from the harbour mud, and fling headlong after shoals of herring, hungry for the cold red blood.

Soon he left his mother's side and rolled with the herd, sleek and rounded and with a smiling eye.

Their leader was the old grey-headed Arran, wise and heavy-browed, scarred with the wounds of many battles, careful of his happy herd.

But as the years passed he grew slower, and the greyness spread over his body; he found he could no longer be the father of his herd, and the young bulls ranged relentlessly at his flanks. One day Phoca, the strongest among them, challenged him and took his place, and Arran fell away from the herd, making his

slow way alone through the seas to die. And Barra his son ran close to the new leader, awaiting his season.

Rolling down the sea lanes the herd gambolled past the Welsh headlands and rounded the islands of the west. Heading in from the Bishop Light they ran close to the outer isles, surprising Grypus, the grey seal, on his throne of rock. Grypus beat his flipper angrily and barked a warning to his wives, who shuffled higher up the ledges to their pups, rolling and huffing in their haste to escape from the water and the hunting porpoise pack. Turning eastward, the herd was some miles off the Wolf when Barra became aware of a vast unease, a taste, a smell of something acute and dangerous in the waters behind. The singing of the water had ceased, something was rising like thunder from the depths; something that cut the seas away like a knife, and came black and headlong in a roar of water.

Barra's fear tainted the sea around him, and several of the herd dived sharply with him, away from Phoca, and fled downwards into darkness, their fear twittering like birds. They were not with the main herd when Orca the black killer smashed into them.

They splintered under the impact, and the dreaded Orca chopped among them like a vast black hound, his little eye insane with double lust; with the savagery of the world of beasts and of the world of fish beneath the water; the savagery of the killer-whale. He ripped and tore until he swam through red water, and Phoca, bitten through the spine, sank bubbling numbly into the depths, whining as he slowly drowned in his own blood. When they came together again it was a pitiful small herd that limped on up-Channel, some with great wounds that looked as though cut out by spades, some with hanging tattered flesh and one old female with her flipper torn away. And Barra passed to their head and became their leader; the father of the little herd, nursing them on their painful way, careful of the pups and females, fierce towards the upstart bulls; a wise ruler in his small water-world. They followed the fine ships of those days, the tall windships, the exulting clippers, who raced the sun around the world. Foaming up-Channel with every stitch singing, the fighters of Cape Horn returned to their home ports, and beside them rolled the porpoises, the travellers of the sea.

It was on a cold March morning, when the wind blew hard from the west in a flurry of ice-blue sky and shouting blue water, that the *Queen of Heaven* entered the Channel approaches, and running rails under she creamed past the Lizard, thundering to her press of sail. The loveliest of her line and generation, she was so beautiful that old sailors told of her in later years with the dreaming eyes of lovers; and where some carried devils in their hearts, and some cried out with unquiet spirits, and some killed their master and half their crew before they killed themselves, the *Queen of Heaven* was a sweet ship—a great ship.

On that shouting March day Barra and his herd ran close to her up the Channel, and her crew came into the bows to watch them as they played.

As the great forefoot dipped and rose Barra would let her touch his tail for a moment before effortlessly increasing his pace. He dived beneath her and came up to windward, seeing the clean and lovely lines of her hull surging above him, cutting through green water and leaving a hissing silver trail smoking like a comet.

Over the years Barra and his herd greeted the *Queen of Heaven* as she entered English waters after her long flight from the ends of the world, and the sailors came to look for their approach as a sign of homecoming.

Sometimes she would roll in greasy calms off Start Point and remain idle for the day, until an evening wind breathed again; then joyfully she would begin to move, whispering over the water, and lean into the night for a quiet run home, the porpoise pack rolling with her. And sometimes she would come glorious, carrying all sail to a strong sou'westerly, storming past the Lizard in a burst of white water, her jib boom singing a strange song of wandering horizons, of her flight around the Horn, of her long-awaited landfall.

Such a ship was the *Queen of Heaven*: a perfect union of man's craftsmanship with wind and water—but her soul, her ship's soul, her own until her ending.

And Barra grew slowly grey with years, and one day he left the pack and went on his way alone. He was tired with the efforts of piloting his large herd, of the constant vigilance and the unrelenting challenge of the younger bulls.

And as he grew old the ships of sail became fewer, and the pump and bellow of engines and the blackness of smoke heralded a future age: an age of clanging iron and thrashing propellers. The new iron ships thrust aside the wind and fouled the seas with soot and rainbow-oils, and Barra fled from their presence.

He could now accompany the few remaining windships for only a little while; but their crews still looked for him as they entered the Channel reaches and became fond of the 'white-headed porpoise' who travelled alone.

His speed was gone and he could no longer keep up his effortless run by the flying forefoot. He grew faint for air when pressed, and one day he left the sweetness of the sea to rest in muddy harbours. And one by one the windships went from the sea.

Lying under the sodden branches of half-submerged oaks, Barra waited for straying mullet or a sickly salmon, and ignobly hustled to a grimy kill in the brown waters of shallow creeks. He rubbed his itching back on the keels of boats at anchor, listlessly scratching like a farmer's pig to rid his body of the harbour lice.

One day a great toothed whale, old and desperate with sickness, crept into the little harbour and rolled despairing beside the quay to a slow and monstrous death; such a vastness, such an enormity of death that dismayed the people watching on the quayside, and filled their hearts with pity for the stricken giant.

And Barra felt a great need to go from the unhealthy waters of the harbour, for he felt the spirit leaving him, and he wished his ending to be in the clearness of the sea, in the truth of green water, in his beginning. He lay on the outgoing tide and, slipping past the last rocks of the land, he reached out to sea as a traveller eagerly approaches home.

Through a night of running cloud, with a sprinkling of rain flighting down in the wind-gusts, Barra drifted quiet in his loved sea lanes.

Dawn came yellow-bellied, with a streak of livid green where the sun should be, and the wind swung south-east and whined uneasily. All through the morning the sea rose and the wind harrowed the crests and roared in to savage the land, and under the lash of the wind the sea smoked. Barra swam slowly below the storm, only rising into the troubled surface waters to blow. The shrieking wind and flying spray bewildered him, and he found difficulty in breathing through the whip of water. The smaller ships had run for safety, and by evening the storm was at its height.

Two ships only could be seen from the Lizard station—one an ocean tug, the other all that remained of the *Queen of Heaven.*

Ploughing and veering behind her small jailer, chained like a dog, the *Queen of Heaven* floundered on her last journey to a knacker's end in a breaking-yard. Stripped of her pride, she heaved and plunged, forced unwillingly against the wind which had exalted her in all her former victories.

The small tug laboured against tide and wind, shaken by the erratic plunging of her great prisoner as a rabbit is shaken by a hound. To the watchers at the Lizard her task became unbearable, and with relief they saw her cast off all lines and steer out to sea, to the safety of deep water, leaving the great hulk to drive ashore. As Barra forced himself up to gasp into the gale, the *Queen of Heaven* roared down upon him, and his old eyes were too dim to see her ravaged superstructure. He saw only the lovely waterlines of her hull as she swept by; and suddenly his heart leaped with a great shaft of happiness like sunlight, and he took his accustomed place by her side as she raced towards the land. Intent as a hawk for the kill she flew at the raging rocks, and to the watchers on shore it was as though a terrible voice cried from her—the cry of a ship that has lost her soul. . . .

In the calm of morning they found her.

All that could be called ship had vanished. Only a great mass of broken wood lay on the beach of the little cove, and broken wood washed gently in the weary tide.

And they found, cast high up on the beach and lying across the shattered golden figurehead of the *Queen of Heaven*, the body of an old white-headed porpoise.

Look at him, they said. He must have followed the old ship home. Look at the way he's smiling—it's almost human, they said. And as they turned away up the beach the sun rode out from behind the clouds and a crow dropped heavily to the water's edge, and strutting along the sands began to peer and prod amongst the wreckage.

Breed Unknown

Johnny Whistler was a minor poet, somewhat exquisite and with an *élite* coterie of fellow minor poets, those with poetic aspirations and the various intellectual oddities who gather in some of the better known London pubs and discuss intellectual problems with high voice, little shrieks and limpid gestures. He was also a surprisingly fine painter, with a sensitivity and economy of line and a personal style by which you knew his work at once: 'That's a Whistler!'

Although he was a party-giver of liberal and eccentric proportions, he lived in between a very solitary life on the bottom floor of a large house near the Bayswater Road, with a Russian Blue cat which he worshipped. The cat felt no answering emotion. It had a baleful squint and a spiteful disposition.

Johnny was very proud of this cat, which was a deep blue colour with velvet fur like a mole's and a long elegant body like the Egyptian cats who stare from their thousand years in bronze and stone.

If he was asked why not Siamese he would say, 'But, my dear, *everyone* has them these days. . . .'

At the back of the house there was a derelict shed filled with gardening tools, a rusty printing press and sacks of mousy papers which a previous tenant had left behind, and a wasteland of weeds and bricks, old dustbins, a radiator, kettles and a very fine old walnut tree which alone listened to the season's passing. Johnny had tidied half the shed for himself, and stored his coal and motor-scooter in it, the cat went for personal reasons into the weeds under the walnut tree, and the tree itself was a source of constant reproduction in most of Johnny's canvases, with its thick, twisted branches. But that was as near as Johnny himself got to what he fervently called 'wild Nature', in a tone which implied that she was waiting for him in the weeds and would rend him to shreds at a whim. . . . Nature to Johnny was something to be avoided if possible; it was messy and usually wet and you got grubby and cold . . . and then, somehow, 'it' became 'she' and then terrible, orgiastic.

He might never have seen the horse that morning if his cat had not stayed out so long that he went to the back window to see if she was all right. There was no sign of her, but standing under the walnut tree was a horse. He could hardly believe it. A horse. How had it got in? Oh Lord, it had probably gone through the shed and done God knows what to the pink scooter. He would go and open the garage doors and shoo it out through them into the street. But who owned it? Shouldn't he ring the police? Oh dear, was it savage? He knew they kicked, and he had read of stallions' teeth . . . it was all very well writing 'Odes to Pegasus' . . . the last one was very descriptive and powerful, he felt—but a horse in the flesh . . . a lot of flesh; how tall a horse is really . . . was another matter. He fluttered from the window and ran down the back steps, opened the garage doors from both sides, then, walking as delicately as the blue cat, went behind the horse and at a safe distance took out his handkerchief, waved it frantically and cried 'Shoo!' And clicked his tongue.

He felt extraordinarily silly in the morning warmth, particularly as the horse turned and looked at him and did not, as he'd hoped, bolt decently for the street and become someone else's problem.

He had to admit that seen closely it was a beautiful animal, and it stood so proudly that it seemed not to notice the weeds that came up nearly to its belly, and its eyes . . . Never had he seen an eye like that before; it was full and dark and shone as though alight from within; there was true pride there, fire and generosity, and—yes, almost compassion. It was a look that you never saw in another man's eye; Johnny realized that he had always longed to see this once in a lifetime. . . . Even he could see that this was no ordinary horse; perhaps it was an Arab; he knew they were highly bred and delicately boned like this horse, with a neck curved so perfectly that it appeared sculpted rather than made of flesh, and a mane which fell like a waterfall down to the shoulders, and rippled and danced at every turn of the small exquisite head. The horse turned, and stepped towards him. He saw flared nostrils which might seize the wind, ears as sharp as Damascus knives, and the great wings which the horse now unfolded and stretched around him.

With a quick shake of his head, the snow-white horse struck the ground three times, and up through the weeds bubbled a thin trickle of water which rapidly fountained and spread, reaching its own level in rushes and jerks until it disappeared under the neighbouring fence. From there it continued through two gardens and out through another garage into the street. Johnny was horrified; a kettle bobbed by on the now fast-running stream, and the walnut tree was as though it was a willow on a river bank. He must get this wretched animal out of sight before the complaints started; a Hippocrene on Helicon was fine—but *here*! All he could expect was a writ for damages from the L.C.C.

He could see now how the horse had come in; he'd flown. Really it was quite an honour, but he'd have to get the horse somehow to one of the parks, or Hampstead Heath perhaps, his wings covered by a blanket or something, and hope he'd take off from there and go and start a Hippocrene for someone else. Meanwhile hide him.

Forgetting all about getting grubby he stacked and repacked and swept the shed, and the horse, as though knowing what was wanted, folded his great wings along his back and stepped into it.

The next day or two were hell for Johnny; a thick fog came

down and he could not move the horse as planned. He'd no idea what a horse ate, and although he let the animal out once or twice at night when no one was about, it did not touch the weeds and rank grass.

The civil engineers arrived in force, and various local departments tried to stop the flow of water which they said was a spring, although why it had appeared so suddenly and in such profusion was astounding.

Meanwhile Johnny let out his great horse every night to graze as he hoped, and fed him porridge oats in such quantities that his dietary habits became a source of wonderment and discussion in the neighbourhood. This continued for three days, but on the third night the horse had vanished. Johnny was astonished; he had done everything for the ungrateful animal and was even considering holding a party and leading all his friends down to the shed to fling open the door and show off his magnificent capture, and bask in the exclamations and uproar. He became aware that the silvery sound of the bubbling waters had ceased: the spring had gone. With a queer twist of regret he turned back to the house. You're a bloody fool, Johnny, he told himself. Next time tell the authorities to go to hell, and preserve the sacred stream as you would the rarest jewel, and for God's sake find out how to keep a horse properly. But in his heart he knew there never would be another time. On the steps he called: 'Puss, Puss, Puddy, Puddy', and the blue cat shot past him into the house.

Seamus O'Day was out cold.

It could have hailed hailstones as big as buckets on him and he would have felt nothing; but it did not as some of his friends had brought him home, slung between them like a dying porpoise, with his knees bending at every step like an ape's and his feet taking short runs on their own before sliding sideways like a puppet's when the string breaks. Seamus was a moderately successful playwright who thought of himself more as a poet. He could twist words fine with a Blarney accent that shrouded all faults in a Celtic twilight of personal charm and rolling Rs. He was the blue-eyed boy or the biggest rogue out, according to your personal preference, but it was impossible to ignore him; you either loved or loathed him—there were no halves where Seamus was concerned.

His wife Bridie succeeded fairly well in ignoring him, which increased his indigenous thirst enormously, so that 'home' became anywhere where Bridie was not, and as it was prodigious, 'home' also meant any sort of licensed premises. The only trouble was, inevitably, money; his work was now on in those select theatres with more honour to their names than financial success, and Seamus sorely needed finances for his liquid and spiritual desires which were closely related to, and balanced by, each other. Unfortunately, instead of drinking between periods of work—which one well-known poet described as being the only thing possible when the elation and struggle of writing are over and the long period of uncreative, unrewarding depression sets in—Seamus drank unrelentingly before work, throughout it and after, with the consequence that his talent, which was considerable, flowed in and out like the tide, but mostly away. Hospitals saw him come and go, but like Tennyson's brook his thirst went on for ever; and after perhaps a month hunching about like a sick hen on the wagon, there would be a sidle towards the nearest pub, a quick look, a faster shuffle, and finally a glad gallop; and the cry of Brian Boru going into battle was a pale effort beside the roar of Seamus O'Day hitting the bottle again. . . .

It was midday when Seamus surfaced into a fog of consciousness; Bridie had gone to work as usual. She was so used to finding his snoring form on the living-room sofa that she took no more notice of him than you would of the sofa itself, and if you didn't know when the creature would awaken, sure, what was the point of making him any breakfast at all? It would be either stone cold or burnt to a cinder according to where you left it, and either would be wrong to himself there, with a head on him like a bear in a bee-hive.

Seamus never bothered to look at himself in the hall mirror; it was a familiar and repulsive sight and one best ignored. He flopped into the kitchen, turned on the gas for coffee, and opened the back door for milk. With a groan he held on to the door frame with one hand and bent carefully towards the bottle on the step. As he straightened he saw the horse. 'Jesus,' he said softly. Then he saw the wings.

Now would you be horse or angel, he thought, and taking the milk bottle into the kitchen he put it down on a table and then went to the step again to see if the horse—or angel—was still there. Horse it was. Now there's a thing, said Seamus O'Day. A fine horse like that was worth some money. Oh, indeed he was. It did not occur to him even to doubt that this winged visitor was the beloved of the Muses, but a draught from the Hippocrene meant little to a man with a taste for something stronger. Undoubtedly there would be a reward out for this creature; if not, it was easy to invent damages of various kinds. Or a zoo or circus would pay good money for such a rarity as a winged horse, and if he could hold the animal until he could make arrangements, Bridie need not know, and he'd have such a ball on the proceeds that *Finnegans Wake* would be a parochial whist drive compared to the hooley Seamus O'Day would be having. Television appearances too: himself and the horse. It therefore pained him exceedingly to see the horse suddenly stretch and lift its wings and leap lightly over the fence into a neighbour's garden, where it began to graze on the lawn. Seamus immediately rang the radio and television stations, the police and anyone else he could think of; at least they could see the beast right there in that blessed garden, even if he couldn't lay hands on it himself. Three times the horse struck the grass of the Dublin suburb, and the same crystal-clear spring welled up. Seamus thought of the rope in the attic, left there by friends whose car had once broken down, and he rushed upstairs to get it. He nearly broke his neck coming down, and still trying to tie a slipknot in one end of the rope he fell down the back steps and heaved himself over the fence. But the horse had gone and there was no spring to be seen. Cars arrived from different directions, but the drivers saw only a man babbling of winged horses, and crying and cursing as he was led away by the police and rushed to hospital.

Seamus O'Day remained there for three months.

The doctors said it was inevitable.

The next human being to see the winged horse was an insignificant greyish little man, Henry Jones, who filled up greyish government forms all day and 'dabbled in poetry', as he apologetically murmured when asked about any hobbies, old man, at his local or at the tennis club. His wife, a bird-like little woman, pecked at small canvases and 'dabbled in oils'.

The great horse came to rest on the lawn by their summer-house, and caused them much consternation and argument as to what to do.

The slender hoof poised and struck and the spring fountained up as before. This must be done properly, thought Henry Jones, and he duly signed the form relating to the Importation of Horses Act, 1869. Under the heading 'Breed' he wrote 'Unknown', and hurried out to post it to the Ministry of Agriculture. On the way he inspected the damage done to the dahlias by the spring. On his return the horse and the spring had vanished. Henry Jones sighed with relief and set about re-staking the sodden dahlias, and Mrs Jones chirped and twittered and produced her *pièce de résistance*, her masterpiece—even if she said so as shouldn't. It depicted a fluffy indistinct mass slightly like a white woollen butterfly, and which she said was rather modern, really—really rather abstract. 'Horse at Dawn.' And congratulated herself that she had got out of the difficulty of producing a

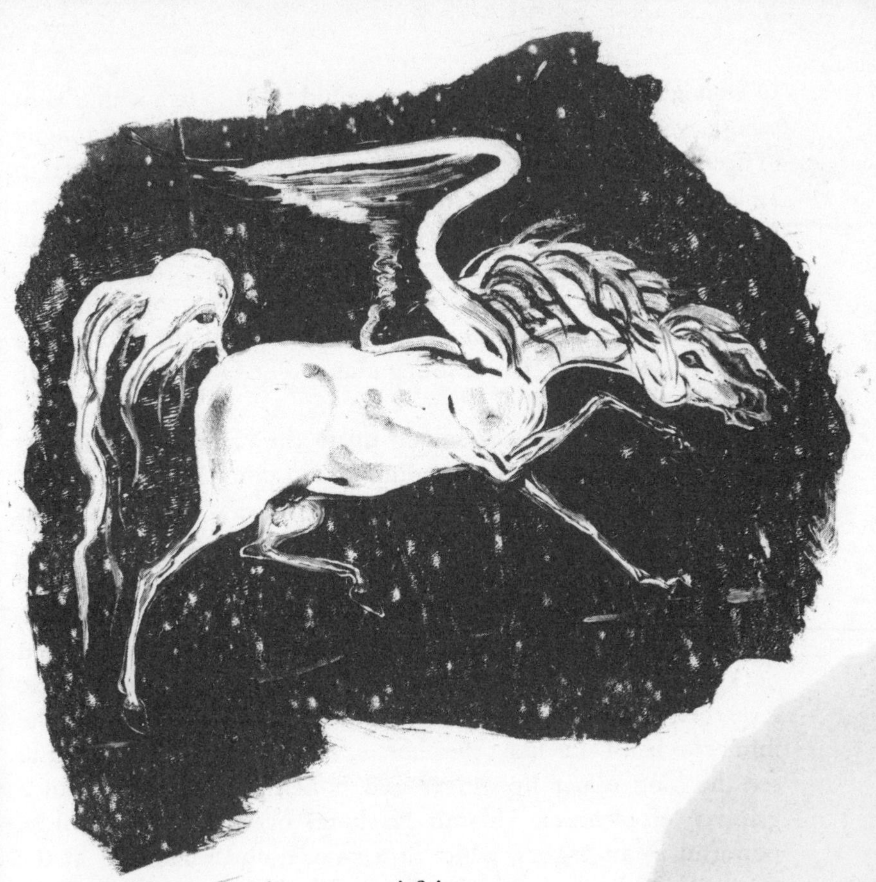

recognizable one in the most satisfying way.

Tadgh O'Donoghue was near his eightieth year. The O'Donoghue was a poet, his father was a poet and his father before that, and for as far as they could trace. This was long; there had always been bards and poets among the O'Donoghues since the days of the Giants. The O'Donoghue himself was the last of them. He published nothing, but to his cabin came all kinds of men, young men and old, to hear him speak and tell his tales: the old tales of secrets, of beliefs, of magic and the speaking of wisdom which is the true poetry. He had never married, had the

O'Donoghue, and sure no woman would want to live with a man whose eyes carried the gaze of eagles and who spoke with a tongue of fire. No woman, unless she was a goddess—and they are dead in Ireland now—could understand the ways of the heart and mind of the O'Donoghue, who held his eighty years as a mountain carries a cloud, lightly.

His white hair and beard were like snow on a mountain, and his tall figure—he was taller than most men of the West—was scarcely less upright than a young man's. The O'Donoghue; there was only the one.

When the great horse stepped up to the cabin door, the first light of morning still lay on the mountains and the lake, and the spiders' webs on the fuchsia bushes held the dew and sparkled as though so many strings of diamonds were hung on them.

When the O'Donoghue opened the door and saw the horse before him, shining as though it carried the morning on its wings, he was not surprised. He ran a horseman's hand up the curved neck and gently lifted a strand of the snowy mane back into place, scratched his visitor's withers and was touched to see that the immortal beast was like other horses, ticklish there, and smiled to see the long upper lip quiver and bunch and draw back in a grimace of pleasure. He ran his hand over the folded wings, powerful as an eagle's, white as a swan's, and marvelled at the great eye of the horse, shining out at him like the moon from the lake's surface.

Then the O'Donoghue prepared a bed of heather and moved the ass to one side of the shelter at the back of the cabin, and put down an armful of his own hay, cut from the small field up the mountain. The great horse went into the shelter and lay down. The O'Donoghue left the door open so that his guest was free to go if he wished, and went about his tasks for the day.

The hoof of the winged horse again commanded the spring, clear as crystal from the limestone of the mountain, and it still runs today. Where? Now that would be telling.

The winged horse still dwells with the O'Donoghue, and every seven years, in the spring of the year, a great salmon swims up the stream to its source close to the O'Donoghue's door. He is left in peace, for this is the salmon of knowledge, and the O'Donoghue already knows a great deal and is too wise to wish to take him.

Where in Connemara, do you say? As I said before, that would be telling.

The Silver Bullet

NO ONE knew the age of Genty Lovelace. For as long as folk could remember she had lived in the old wooden hut under the downs. No one could remember her as a young woman, or when she had first come to live there; year after year she had lived alone with the hills, white-haired and her face as brown and wrinkled as a windfallen apple. And the surrounding blue-eyed villagers found her gaze disturbing and strange, for Genty's eyes were as black as the berries on the elder tree.

As old as the hills they called her; and she would have laughed and said it was so. Green as the eyes of a jealous woman were the hills that Genty loved, rolling southerly and in summer drowsy with the content of bees. No road led to her house, only the sheep tracks lined the face of the hills as the years had worn the face of the woman among them. The Down sheep drifted all the day past her door until evening, when the great flocks would climb to where the dew-ponds lay quiet under the moon. Quiet, and silver like a coin in a gypsy's hand. In summer the larks praised the heavens in a radiance of singing, and flocks of little finches rattled in the thorn bushes by Genty's house. In winter, only the finches and wrens stayed to fidget in the bushes, when the falcon swept to his kill on the grey wings of the north wind. And when the black wind came in from the east one robin only remained at Genty's door and told in a sad small voice of the cold that will come, of the life that will go. And the old woman, on hearing him lament, would carry out a saucer of scraps to make sure her tiny ruffled friend would not go hungry to his bed in the thorn bushes.

Thus the seasons passed over the face of the hills, but they were unchanged and their face was serene, for the wisdom of the centuries lay upon them.

Genty had no love for her fellow men, her heart was gentle only for the wild creatures which she loved as though they had been her children, and the people of the villages, not understanding why she should want to live so far away and alone with the hills, were afraid of her. And, being the way of those who fear what they cannot understand, they called her a witch. The one day in the week when she walked with her two large baskets to the village the children would run in front of her, taunting her, and few would wish her a good day. She was 'queer'; she wasn't of their ordered ways, of shopping and gossip, feeding the smug cat, twitching the curtains to see who went by and why; of the frenzied scrubbing of the sinful doorsteps.

Some hurried by with a mutter into the pavement, some stared into the draper's window earnestly as she approached, and when she had passed they turned and hated her with their eyes.

Genty would sell whatever she had in her baskets as soon as possible, and leave the village as quietly as the last leaf will leave a tree on a day of frost.

Sometimes she had a young cockerel to sell, or some flowers from the little garden behind her house, or a few small cheeses from her two goats. There were two old ladies who lived in a pleasant brick house near the church, and they always bought Genty's cheeses, for they had lived as young girls in Switzerland, and it took them back to those dear departed days when they had laughed without fear of tears and where everyone had eaten goat's-milk cheese.

They paid Genty well, and were the only people in the village who gave her any kindness, and always they would gently press her to take tea with them in the high white drawing-room overlooking the small lawn and the church wall, and the scent of roses seemed to come out from the bricks of the house even in winter.

Genty would sit stiffly upright on the rose-chintz sofa with her boots close side by side on the carpet, and drink the pale tea they offered her in a fragile cup, her brown hand unaccustomed to holding anything so delicate—except perhaps a frightened bird. The dying partridge she had found, after Farmer Stevens' shooting party had gone by, reminded her of the cup. They were both so small, so light and fragile. The plaintive little dog would press against her skirt and shiver with gratitude when she looked down at him; and when it was time to go the two old ladies would wave her down the scented path and make the gardener cut a special rose for her, which he did as reluctantly as if cutting off his own hand.

Then Genty would buy a few things in the village to last her for another week and set off for the downs late in the afternoon. And the two old ladies would turn and sigh, and close the white front door with its big brass knocker, and putting on their spectacles one would take up her knitting and the other a book from the library, while a young officer in a long-forgotten uniform stared eternally heroic from his yellowing frame on the mantelpiece, and the gardener on the lawn outside muttered into the rose bushes and glared at the empty stalk which had carried Genty's bloom.

For three miles Genty would have to walk the road, until she reached a cool gathering of beech trees at the top of a steep hill. They cast a shadow so deep and tranquil that travellers had been known to rest beneath their branches and sleep away a day and a night, so great was the peace in that place.

A white dusty sheep track led up on to the downs from the beech grove, and Genty would climb slowly with the summer-blue scabious and tender harebells swinging in the hill wind, and her heart would sing with the riding larks, for she was come home.

No sheep ran in panic from her; no lambs flung away like a handful of blown paper at her approach, for they all knew Genty well, and knew the sweetness in her heart for all creatures. They called to her as she passed; their quick light eyes watched her kindly and their questing noses touched the scent of her.

Their small minds nodded with the pleasure of seeing her go by, and no fears raced to confound them into anxious movement.

Genty would reach her house at last and set her kettle on the fire to make her tea—strong brown tea that rushed down the throat in a cheerful gulp; proper tea, thought Genty, not that poor pale stuff the two old Miss Hendys made, poor dears. Looked more like the piss of a nanny-goat, and hardly warmed your tongue, let alone the heart.

And Genty would sigh and stretch out her boots to the fire's glow and feel how good it was to be home, like a snail in its well-known shell, while the house darkened slowly into dusk and the hour of the nightjars was come. With a clap of wings they darted into the valley like sudden thoughts in a sleeping mind, to crouch among the dreaming sheep and begin spinning the mantle of night.

Genty would light her candle and watch her small fire fade, while her young magpie flew up to spend his night on top of the old clock in a corner of the room, settling his head beneath one wing, taking a last quick black look all round; and with a sneeze and a chuckle fall asleep with his long tail hanging down the face of the clock.

Genty would share her supper as usual with the old rough dog who came stiffly into the house as soon as night approached. Turned out by one of the farms because he was of no use to them, the big brown dog had lived for fourteen years with Genty, and now being old he wished for very little save the small delights of sitting in the sun, Genty's hand on his head and her word for his heart. When they had finished a crust would be left on the table for the magpie and the small window left open at the top if he wished to fly into the morning, then Genty would blow out the candle and silence would fall over the little house.

There were some nights when sleep would not come to Genty,

for she was an old woman and no longer needed the hours of the young, and when this happened she would leave the house and walk out over the downs. The old dog would listen at the door until he lost the sound of her going, then return to his place by the hearth and lie quietly awaiting her return, dozing but never quite asleep in case she should come.

And on every night that she walked upon the hills under the stars a big hare would come from behind the house and lope after her over the downs.

When dawn came, and the first small wind that heralds the day passed over the grass, the big hare would run down the sheep track back to her form behind the house, awaiting the sun's rising with her coat dark with dew and her long legs pressed into the wet grasses.

And Genty, returning, would softly close her door. The old rough dog would rise and question her with his anxious eyes, and the magpie would stir and stretch out a thin black leg, scratch his head and prepare his feathers for the day.

While the kettle boiled he would seize his crust and fly to the table to knock it into small pieces against the teapot. Then sidling to the window he would look out, wheezing and chuckling down his throat, and fly into the morning with a shout and a clatter.

And Genty would sit at her door in the fresh sunlight and hope this would not be one of the days when Farmer Stevens would come and bully her with his overbearing ways and his threats to evict her from her house. Genty had no fear of Farmer Stevens, but his anger spoilt her day, and the sun never seemed so warm after he had been and shouted at her.

But Farmer Stevens hated Genty. Her presence in the valley was like a thorn in his shoe, and he constantly trod hard on the thorn and his mind simmered with resentment over the years. He owned the big Overlong Farm down by the village, and his lands ran up to the edge of the downs. For years he had wanted Genty's little house, which stood on a plot of rough ground just inside his boundary. But the previous owners of Overlong Farm, liking the hermit-like old woman, had never troubled her, and under a clause in the deeds of the farm Farmer Stevens was unable to claim the house until she died, or moved.

He had a prosperous summer trade with campers, but Genty's house would have let for a grand sum, and his wish was to put caravans all down the valley.

But the years went by and, bluster and threaten as he would, Farmer Stevens could make no impression on the old woman.

Old bitch'd live for ever, it'd seem. Wouldn't be surprised if she weren't a witch. Shepherd Johns over to Chambourne swore he'd seen her turn into a hare. She hadn't seen him neither; too busy up to her foul trade.

The thoughts in Farmer Stevens' mind turned black. Another thing, whenever he'd been out with a party trying for a few hares, damned if the old hag weren't always on ahead; deaf seemingly and blind as well to all signals, and where she went a great hare'd spring up. And well out of range, thanks to her. And then she'd vanish clean off the earth. He'd seen her with his own eyes—one minute she was there, the next she'd gone and not a trace of her:

only a big hare going on over the next ridge. . . . Damn and blast the old witch, for that was surely what she was. And Farmer Stevens laid down a curse in his heart for Genty.

Turns into a hare, does she? . . . then we'll know what to do about that. . . . A silver bullet's the answer, but silver it must be . . .

So Farmer Stevens waited for the night when Genty, feeling no use for sleep, should walk over the downs, and many nights he sat cold under the stars and quiet with dew; patiently under the singing stars, while the moon walked, but Genty slept. Then came the dark nights when the downs seemed to stir and creep in around him, filled with little tittering voices spiteful and mocking, and in the mornings the farm-hands would wonder at their master's haggard face. And on some of those black nights when the soul lies chilled and dark there came the host of the hares thundering and stamping all around Farmer Stevens, and so great was the unease in his heart that he fancied he heard them singing with voices high and silver, like the voices of the stars.

But he waited on. Then came the night of the full moon, when Genty's house shone white, and the silent man sat on, quiet as time.

And suddenly he saw a great hare who raced out from behind the house, leapt over the chalk path and danced upon the hillside. And a hundred hares sprang up all around, pouring past him like a pack of devils, the big hare running with them, and the moon's delight in their eyes.

Over the rise they leapt thundering; then the quiet crept back to the waiting man. The moon paled and sank and over Farmer Stevens fluttered the small dark wind of dawn. The night of the hares was past. As the hills grew again with the returning light Farmer Stevens slid in the silver bullet and, kneeling on one knee, rested the rifle on the other. The big hare came over the rise with the dawn, and as she jumped on to the white path he fired.

The hare leapt with a small cry of despair and the demented echo tore out of the heart of the hills.

Farmer Stevens stumbled heavily down to where the hare had fallen, but when he reached the place there was nothing—nothing. Panting, he ran towards the little house, and as he ran he heard a dog howling inside.

He flung open the door and cried with a bitter fear as the magpie flew into his face with a scream. It was as though the black soul of the witch had attacked him, and he cowered down in the doorway as the bird flew cursing into the morning and the old dog with the broken heart called on his gods in his distress.

In the only chair lay Genty, and she was dead. Farmer Stevens in a tumult of fear and guilt gazed at the old woman, shaking. He could smell his fear—stinking like a fox from his armpits. He had killed the witch, but he must remove the traces of his murder. Silver'd melt in a high heat. Set fire to the house. Burn the witch.

He kicked out the remains of the fire over the floor and ran weeping from the house as though the dead woman might yet pursue him. . . .

The inquest returned a verdict of accidental death, and no one could tell how it happened.

The old woman had perhaps died of heart failure, or an attack of some sort, and had fallen into the fire. The house was wooden . . . it hadn't taken long.

Pity about the old dog, they said; old women shouldn't be allowed to live all alone like that.

But, unknown to Farmer Stevens, a hare died that day, stretched cold in her form behind the black place where the little house had been, with a silver bullet in her heart.

And from that day everything went wrong with Overlong Farm. The rooks, which from time beyond reckoning had lived in the elms around the farmhouse, deserted even the village, and pestilence fell upon the fine herd that had taken Farmer Stevens so many patient years to build up.

The fields reeked as the pride of his life burned away in great pits; the finest cattle piled one upon the other and burning as fiercely as the house of Genty Lovelace. And never had there been such a plague of hares. They ruined all the fields of Overlong Farm, and a great army came down nightly from the hills and nibbled and chiselled until only the bare earth remained.

Farmer Stevens never saw his farm or herds rise again from the ashes of disaster. They found him dead one winter's afternoon. It seemed that as he went to shut a gate his gun had gone off, and although he was not killed outright the shock and the winter's cold had done the rest. He had tried to crawl for home like a stricken dog; the marks were there, heavy and snail-like among the dead leaves.

His cowman found him as dusk came cold with November over the fields.

Horrible job, he said. All around the body it looked as though hundreds of hares had chased and stamped in a great circle, and as he approached a magpie had lifted heavily away from the dead man's face—a face pitted by savage thrusts from a long black beak, and from which the eyes were missing. Today not a hare remains upon the green hills above Overlong Farm; they have all vanished, and in the little valley there is only grass and the larks rising where once stood the house of Genty Lovelace.

Only the hills remember the time when a great company of hares danced with their eyes bright with the moon-madness, and when an old, old woman walked upon them as light as a young hill hare.

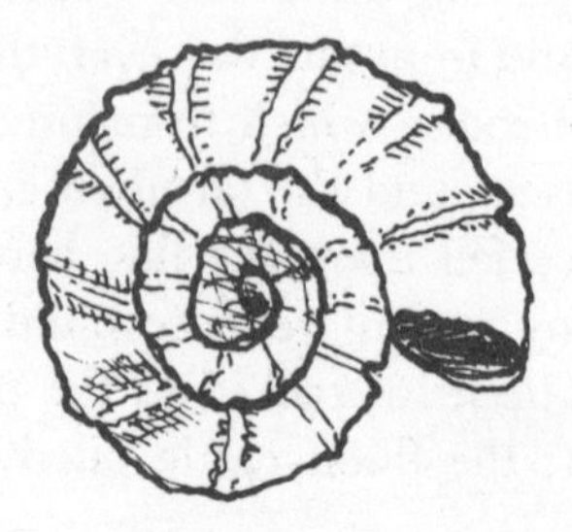

The Seagull

HE SHOOK her savagely until her eyes rolled; they struggled against the table and her hand knocked over the flowered teapot. At the crash she twisted away and they faced each other, breathing hard. She had no more energy for hate. The teapot had been her mother's; it was one of her treasures. No feeling came.

'You bitch,' he said quietly without rancour. 'Next time——'

'Well, what about next time, what about it?'

'I warn you this.' He meant it and she hated him, hated herself more. She raged silently. 'I'm not coming back, I've told you. I'd rather die.'

He said this so slowly, almost in a tone of wonder; he looked at her as you might look at a poisonous plant, or a crushed animal, with a kind of uncomprehending horror. No, not uncomprehending, that was the trouble; he knew too much. He would never be beguiled again. Never.

He took his jacket from the door and pulled on the navy cap. They looked at each other. He went out and shut the door quietly. The latch clicked; his footsteps were light, not as though a man was walking out there on the quay, but the quick, homeless noise that your eyes rather than ears pick out as a dog passes by on the street. Quick, light; only he knows where he is going as he passes you, with a quick glance as he crosses the road. He belongs somewhere—must do. But where? His eye is bright, he is a world contained in himself, he sleeps, scratches himself, eats, roams fast, friendly seemingly but aloof, alone.

Suddenly she saw her husband like that dog. It hurt. She went to the sink and wrung out a string cloth, mopped the spilled tea from the table, carried the china to the draining-board, set the table straight and put the papery flowers back into the centre on their plastic mat. Then she stood for a moment looking out of the window to where the funnels of the ships showed in the gaps between the rooftops. She had no more rage, there were no more tears. Almost tenderly she picked up the big teapot, looked at its pink roses and gold-topped lid and hurled it into the sink, and after it everything she could lay hands on. A china fragment flew up and cut her skin under one eye. She felt the small pain, and dabbed at the small blood with her apron. Then she took off the apron, hung it over a chair, looked down at the mixture of china and tea-leaves and went slowly out into the town to the shops.

The months changed. Nothing changed for her. The end of October, November . . . would he be back?—at Christmas?

She couldn't remember when she first noticed the bird; it was there when she put out the washing on the Monday, and she flapped a towel at it as it was near the line, but it only scuttered a pace or two away, or if pressed flew up on to the roof and stared down at her. You often got a seagull or two around, but never one as brazen as this. The blasted bird peered at her through the window, tapped on the glass with its cruel-looking yellow beak and watched her with a baleful yellow eye. No sooner did she open the window and shout at it than it was back, nodding its head and screaming at her. It stood on its wrinkled, yellow-jointed legs and mewed and tapped and screeched, balancing on the ledge with a horrible flapping and beating of its wings. Sometimes it was quiet, and she thought it had gone, but no, it was still there; she had only to look at it and it would start up again . . . the crazy running dance on the ledge, the flapping, the bowing and screaming, and all the time the stern yellow eye unwinking, ruthless. It got so bad she couldn't sleep for thinking of it. In the dark did it go away, to wherever seagulls go at dark, or did it hunch itself up at the window? The thought was horrible; she dared not go and see in case it began to beat and flap out there in the night. It was always there first thing in the morning. Sometimes it wouldn't see her at first, be preening its feathers, but as soon as it saw her movement in the room it would begin its diabolical staring, shuffle and flap.

It seemed always to have been there; it beat at her when she went out to hang the washing; it swooped after her, jeering and flapping, when she went to the shops. At last—on a Monday it was—she opened the window. Carefully she went to the window, pulled down the top half first, then lifted up the bottom. The wind blew in the curtains and the bird flopped heavily down into the room, half jumping, half flying. And jeering.

She brought up the poker, held until now behind her back, and the bird looked up at her, its wings out, its eyes unwavering and knowing. She expected evasion, not defiance; it stopped her for a moment. Then she struck and struck and the bird flopped and tossed around the room like a wind-blown newspaper. Cornering it by the radio, she battered in its head, the reddened poker, plastered with its sticky feathers, bent out of shape.

She dimly heard the bell ring in the hall, the brass top came away in her hand, and the rest of the poker fell heavily, hitting her ankle. With revulsion she stepped quickly away from it, from its point covered with blood, feathers and little pieces of flesh. Trembling, she washed it and her hands at the sink, pulled her hair from her ears, struggled to get herself calm and stop shaking.

Slowly she took the telegram. No, no answer. She hadn't looked at it? No, but there was none. There was never an answer needed. She shut the door and the boy spat and walked away.

15 DECEMBER.

TO: MRS NANCY FARROW, 25 THE QUAYS, NEWBRIDGE.

FROM: H. E. BELLEW, MASTER, S.S. MERIDIAN.

DEEPLY REGRET TO INFORM YOU YOUR HUSBAND MET WITH DECK ACCIDENT, SUSTAINING FRACTURED SKULL. . . .

She placed the still bloody poker in the grate, and going across to the radio she picked up the dead seagull by one wing, and taking it to the window flung it out. Then she shut the bottom half, rearranged the curtains and went to the sink for a cloth. She put soap powder and hot water into the plastic bowl and, kneeling, began to wipe up the blood and feathers from the floor.

The calendar with the kittens on it was in tatters where it had fallen from the wall in her attack on the gull, blood smeared all over their sharp, vacant faces. And this day's date she noticed too, torn across, 15th December. Tomorrow. The date of the telegram. But how could it be. . . ?

Still she knelt in growing horror, as a seagull began to flap and batter at the shut window. It was as white as snow, no mark on it, and its eyes hatefully yellow. Yet she had seen that other broken one where she had flung it: where it now lay under the line of washing.

The Mermaid

SO, STRANGER, you would know of the depths of the sea. But only if you have the seventh sight, will we, the grey ones of ocean, sing you of Atlantic. You must lift the listening shell and summon us, the silken ones, from the waters that roll around the Isles of Fortune. And we will rise up from the valleys of Atlantic, and sing to you of Shoonah, the greatest of the seals that ride on the breasts of the sea, and of Lucia, the daughter of Black Isaac from Benbeary. The pride of Shoonah was lofty as a hillock; he was wise in the ways of fishes, and in the ways of water. He was wise with a great sea knowledge.

The strength within his heart was great as the power of the whale, and his neck rose like a wall from the waters. Yet his eye shone as gentle as the moonlight shines green fathoms under.

Black Isaac fishes no longer from Benbeary, and his hair which once had been black as the back of the pilot whale was now white and tattered like spindrift.

Black hair was a strange thing among the islanders; some said it traced to the great gilded ship from Spain which foundered on the seal rocks off the Isles of Fortune, and one man only saved his soul, a man whose hair was black as the rocks of Benbeary.

The old songs told of a black stranger who had married and settled among the islanders, and there had always been a girl named Lucia in the one family with the black Spanish hair; and Lucia was a southern name unknown to the rest of Benbeary.

Black Isaac had none to love but his daughter Lucia; his wife had died in the year of the great storms, when one of the seal islands had been swept from the sight of men. His boat, which had not known the sea for many years, lay high on the white sands. Away from the waters, with a dry crack her heart had broken, and soon she had died quietly, leaning on her side in the manner of boats when they are forsaken. Black Isaac still made nets for the young men of Benbeary, and Lucia helped him at his work and cared for their small cottage.

Benbeary was the largest among the Isles of Fortune, and the only one inhabited by the fishing families. The other islands were the homes of storm-birds and the seals, 'the people of the sea', as the islanders called them, 'the grey ones'.

The village with its small granite church crouched against the western ocean, and lay so close to the water that on nights of great wind the spray covered the houses, and the churchyard glittered beneath a strange drift of foam which ran before the wind and vanished when the sun came. The villagers called the great rollers that reared out of the west the horses of Atlantic, the white-crested stallions of the sea who galloped upon the islands and covered Benbeary with their foam. Even the gravestones in the churchyard were worn smooth as pebbles by the burden of water so often upon them.

When Lucia walked over the island for provisions, she would go to her mother's grave and sit for a while thinking of the woman she had never known, the mother for whom her heart yearned often. She never had the chance to play like other children. Away on the northern side of Benbeary with her old father she had always the cares and tasks of a woman to face alone. Only when she swam in the waters by her home could she leave her daylight self on the beach like a pile of clothes and take on the spirit of water, the fairy spell of water cast upon her by the sea.

She left no flowers upon the grave, for nothing could rest under the claws of the sea wind, but on fine days she stayed longer, when the churchyard became a sheltered place to rest a little time and as pleasantly warm as a mother's heart.

Black Isaac's cottage lay alone, on one side of a small valley, and sheltered from the gales by high rocks. A spring rose at the front of the cottage, and widened into a small stream which trickled down the valley on to the beach and was lost into the white sands. From the windows Lucia would watch the seas roaring into the little cove on stormy days when the rain was flung like pebbles on the glass, and the wind leaned against the door and forced her to keep inside. She would look out when the darkness came early and wonder how the seals were faring out in the teeth of the sea, where the islands were under green water, and only a plume like smoke showed where they had been. Then she would light the lanterns and shut out the darkness, where the old boat shuddered with each leap of the wind as though troubled by an unhappy memory; but the spirit having gone from her, the old boat no longer felt the claws of the wind or the bruising seas. When their meal was done, Black Isaac would tell Lucia stories of the older days when the fish were many and the boats finer and the young men stronger; stories told by fathers to sons, and mothers to daughters, of the days before memory, when stories were legends —and legends were truths.

He would light his pipe, and with a dreaming eye call up the old things, the things of the past from out of the fire's heart, and Lucia would watch all the vanished years flicker over the old man's face and die again in the greyness of ashes.

'I will tell of the years that have gone, child, when a mermaid came to Benbeary; and she was beautiful.

'She lay upon the white sands and saw one of the young men and her heart desired him. Many times she lured him with a wonderful soft singing down to the water, but each time he felt the coldness of the sea closing upon him he had drawn back and left her, for only when she was singing had she the power to destroy his mind's reasoning. Now the young man loved an island girl, but his heart was drawn away to the white sands where the mermaid lay, and at last he would have to leave the warmth of

the houses and go to her with the glitter of stars in his eyes.

'One night he awoke with a cry of terror, for he was in the sea with no knowledge of how he had gone there, and the mermaid was with him, pulling him deeper, deeper. But she was no longer singing, and he turned to look into her eyes for the first time, and he saw bleak death. He snatched his arm away from her cold grasp, and she rushed upon him barking in her anger. And he saw her lovely mouth hid a row of fishes' teeth—little pointed teeth, cruel as needles.

'Plunging from the sea he ran up the beach towards the village, but as he went he heard her curse Benbeary. Shrieking that she would still have him and all the young men of the island, and so break the heart of every woman in the Isles of Fortune, she sank back into the sea, which boiled as though with the heat of her vengeance.

'The next day there blew up a sudden and terrible storm. Howling out of the west it roared down upon Benbeary, and in it perished all the young men and many of their fathers who were out in the boats at sea. And the lamenting of the women lifted high with the sea-birds.

'And now we say that should a mermaid ever be seen again we must bind up our ears and kill her to save Benbeary from the powers we cannot understand.'

The years passed, and Black Isaac was now so old he could only climb slowly down to the white sands upon fine days, and return a bent and shapeless figure, creeping painfully with Lucia at his side to help him over the house-step. On wet days he sat by the window watching with wandering blue gaze the ways of the sea below, watching the changes on the face of the sea with the understanding of a lover. He was no longer occupied with the things of the day; he slept small sleeps in the sun or by the fire, and his mind wrinkled and moved like the mind of the sea.

Lucia grew tall and beautiful and her black hair fell wild as the tail of a hill pony.

One summer there came blue months of fine weather when the wind walked like a stranger, quiet out of the south. Lucia swam often in the little cove, and became brown as a young wren.

And she loved to go to the white sands when they were changed and rich under moonlight, when Black Isaac was sleeping. She would play and dive in the warm summer water, leaving a trail of silver like the flashing of the dolphin's tail. Sometimes, if she dived down quietly, she would see the little flatfish spurt from the sand beneath her, and the moon rocking on the floor of the sea as though in a cradle.

One night she came to the sands, and under the moon she looked up and thought a little while on the great wonders of such a night. All was richness like velvet, when the moon's spell turned the heart into a changeling.

The curlews piped over the far beaches and the night sighed with the passing of wings.

Lucia stared into the crystal of the waters, and she felt the sea breathing quiet as though with her own breath. When she had swum a little way she turned to watch the cottage shining white in the moonlight, and the valley black in shadow. It was then that she heard the strange voice, a curious and sweet voice, calling her name from the water. '*Lucia . . . Lucia . . .*' And Shoonah, the lord of thc seals, rose soundlessly and gazed at her with gentle eyes. She felt no fear; sensing only the gentleness in the great body rocking quietly in the dark water.

Then he sank beneath her with a huff of breath and she saw his shadow gliding by her feet. Without thought of harm she dived after him, and so they played and rolled and dived together, laughing. Lucia had to surface many times for air, and sometimes there would be emptiness on the sea when she came up, and Shoonah would glide under her and stroke her dangling feet and make her gasp and laugh, or sometimes he would float upon his back and fold his flippers solemnly like the preacher in Benbeary, while the water dripped from his whiskers with a sound like the bells of the Little People.

Many nights they played, and when they had swum enough Lucia would sit and sing to Shoonah, who pulled himself half from the water and listened in an ecstasy. Then he would raise his great round head and sing to her, 'Lucia, Lucia', and Black Isaac would stir uneasily in his sleep as the voice of the seal echoed in the caves of his mind.

As time passed Lucia felt there was no need of hiding their friendship, and so they played upon the beach till daybreak, but when the sun rose no persuasions would keep Shoonah beside her, and he would return to the water, and to his own people far off on the seal islands. One dawn it was so bright and golden that Black Isaac awoke early, and in a half-bewilderment of sleep he looked out at the sun's rising. A great fear fell upon him, for he saw a shape in the water below; a girl with long hair streaming down her back like the kelp, who played and rolled, sporting like a sea animal, and when she dived a tail came out of the sea.

His old mind shook with the fear of his discovery. *The mermaid . . . dear God, the mermaid. . . . Woe to Benbeary this day if she should live to curse us all again. She must return to those black depths who have given her strange birth. . . . The gun, aye, that was it, the gun. . . .*

With fumbling grey hands the old man lifted down the long rifle from the hook above the fireplace, and painfully as a snail made his way down to the beach. His mind darkened and became light again, like clouds passing over the sea, but one thought burned above all others that the mermaid must not live, and there must be no lamenting of the women lifting high with the sea-birds. . . .

He rested the rifle carefully on a rock, and called up all his strength to keep his shaking hands quiet and eye cold as frost. The shot roared out of the rocks and sent the curlews wailing from the far beaches like leaves tossed in a wind. The rifle dropped from the old man's feeble hands, and he fell beside it trembling and crying softly for Lucia to come to him and help him back to the safety of the cottage. He was alone by the wastes of water and the mermaid was dead. He had seen her rolling in her sea-death, like a fish that gasps and turns its useless belly to the sky. And Lucia drifted down, slowly down, aimlessly wandering where the currents willed, and Shoonah dived around her, a great unease in his heart.

He tried to make her see him, touched her and tried to make her laugh, which to him was as pleasant as the sunlight, but when he rose into the air he understood the ways of death. Once he had been fired upon by the strangers from the south, and he had seen some of his kind sinking and drifting beyond life, like Lucia. The crack of the rifle and the smack of the whirring bullet ended all laughter. The same day the sea laid Lucia tenderly upon the white sands, and the curlews rose and left the Isles of Fortune.

For a long time Shoonah drifted with the tides, but the sea, once his friend and his life, held no goodness for him and his heart was laden. His voice echoed among the caves of Benbeary, and the seals—we, the grey ones—mourned with him, for we sing with the voices of the forgotten drowned, and ours is the lament of Atlantic. And Shoonah, the greatest of the seals, cried out his longing, until at last, weakly, his head sank beneath the water and he had no further wish for life.

The body of Lucia lies with her mother in the little churchyard of Benbeary. But only we know far out in the foam of the islands her spirit sings with the voice of a seal. When the black storms of winter come, when the wind harries the spray high over the Isles of Fortune, we ride cold in the barking wastes of water, and in the warmth of a fisherman's house an old crazed man sings alone of a mermaid.

The Red Man of the Boyne

'LIM A SHROYNYA THOMAN NEEDIAS MISLI RILHU. GOSHTA RILHU NEEDIAS, GART LAKINS AND GART SWIBLIS, STAYSH AND KRISH GLOCHI AND KRISH KARBS MUKINYA LIM A SHROYNYA. LASHULEST NEEDHAS YOU COULD MISLI, SKAI AND SLOOFA AND KEN THOMS . . . STAYSH GRADIS NEEDIAS RILHU. . . .'

'By the banks of the Boyne many people go mad. Numbers of mad people, young girls and boys, yes and old men and women, too, dwell near the Boyne. It's the loveliest place where you could walk, with water and wood and houses of great folks . . . but it drives people mad. . . .'

'I'M TELLING you, Liam. I'm telling you—it can't go on. Merciful Jesus, but it can't go on.'

'Well now to be sure, I know, I know.'

How did he know? How could he know, this, his good friend, Liam, who had the world? A good house, a good job and a good woman. And the kids. Six lovely children—four little boys and two girls as sweet as angels.

And himself, Jamie Murphy, with nothing; nothing.

It wasn't as though, like some, he was missing a lung, or like some, too, able to make with a smile or a nod and a whine in the voice, and the shilling is there in the hand. Liam—Jesus, it was funny—thought little of his wife. She loved him. Everything he had satisfied him; he took them all for granted; he was comfortable and warm in the heart the way it goes when there is warmth from the fire, food ready and no fear of either ending. And a woman who loved you. Ah, the occasional spat, the fly-off; but behind, the love, the smile in the eyes. Yes, Liam loved her, he was wrong. He just took her for granted. That was all. She was part of the warmth, the fire, the dinner, the mothering, the washing, the bed. If she was *not* one day—not dead, God forbid, or gone any place—but just *not*, then he'd wake up.

Suddenly he would wake up. First the fear, the animal smell of it, the mindlessness, the sweat running cold down his ribs. The washing in the kitchen, hanging as though they were small people, empty people, waiting, waiting. For what?

The fire still in, red. The kettle, breathing, somehow wistful. The cat looking at him from the chair: the lamp-eyed cat whose heart pities neither screaming man nor screaming mouse.

Just imagine, Liam, my friend, my dear friend. Now bring her back. No, don't open the door, or call up the stairs. Just bring her back. From *not* to *is*. Missed her? O heavenly God. You could do that, Liam, just by a thought, a twist of the mind. Just tilt the invisible balance in which the mind's thoughts are held, take one out and the frail oscillation begins, think again and the balance is even. Just like that, as simple as that. Not, Liam, Liam, not as with mine. Gone, gone, gone, and the word like the great bell for the soul's peace. No word, nothing to tell me of her. Why, why?

Her feelings, her heart. She, who was so kind. The pitiful scraping, asking, trying, breaking. Was that it? She'd never complained. If only she had. But she who was so gentle, and little Kathy. . . . He tried not to think, not to remember; but it was on him again, the tiger of memory, its teeth in his brain, its claws dragging out the crying thoughts, dragging the bleeding tears down his torn cheeks. He found it was his own hands.

Kathy and she asleep together, as though together in the big bed, only their heads were under the water, bright red water. Bath water, still warm, blood warm. . . . He still couldn't turn on the taps of the bath or basin for fear they should run red. . . .

There was no way out. Insanity? You pleaded for release, but there was none; there was no escape through that labyrinth.

The kindness was like a sea around him, the kind voices roared in his ears like the sea. Roared, beat like breakers, and, like the sea, retreated. He pulled the warm blanket of kindness around him, but it was no help. The intention, help, pity. But help took her hand away and you fell; you were better without; pity glazed her own eyes and turned gnawing at her own vitals. Jamie Murphy stood as though at the end of a long road, which had taken him his life to walk, and which suddenly ended a few steps ahead. Ended. Just that. Or else, barely visible, writhed away to one side up a black mountain which was limitless, without footholds, barren. The heart of Jamie Murphy was weary and spent; there was a time, and gladly. But not now. Jamie Murphy could climb no further on life's mountain. . . .

Liam pulled his cap on to his ears. 'Well, I'm for home. Good night all, good luck.' It was a terrible night to be out at all. God help anyone at sea in this. That was a queer tale now, and one he hadn't heard before; almost wish home didn't lie alongside the river. The tinker Barlow could be relied on for a good tale, but the Red Man of the Boyne—well, that he didn't know. Quite a character, old Barlow, and as dark as most tinkers are fair. A decent man too, not one of your rowdy sorts at all. A good, clean-living man; bet his wagons are taking a shaking in this wind. God knows how they managed in weather like this; couldn't light a fire for sure, but then they had a stove of sorts in the vans, could be cheerful enough, and they were used to weather. Still, no joke tonight at the river's edge; bad enough in a house. He thought with pleasure of his home; not far now. He walked fast; some way ahead a figure showed under a street lamp, pale and blurred by the driving rain as though made of yellowish needles. Liam bent his head again to the wind as it hurled the rain against his coat with a sound like thrashing twigs. He and the man ahead were now long since past the boats straining and yawing by the quays, riding high and uneasy on the high-running tide; ships and houses almost on the same level, with the road flooded and the river pushing and gulping at the town bridge.

He chuckled; Mrs Lannery might look out tomorrow morning and find the *Dimity* at the bottom of her garden if things got much worse . . . not that she wasn't used to entertaining a sailor or two, the old——!

The last of the street lights was overhead, now it was darkness as far as the fishing villages at the Head; away to his right the water was beating and spitting over the narrow stone causeway which connected the two banks of the river. . . . Dear God—what was that?

Even as Liam saw the figure staggering against the wind he realized it was Jamie Murphy, and thought he knew what lay in the poor battered heart of the man. 'Jamie! Jamie!' he shouted, and tried to run, but the wind was so great his legs felt as though he was pushing through water, and his words hurt in his mouth. At the edge of the causeway he stood for a moment, feeling his trouser legs and shoes full of the river; peering under his hands he could just see Jamie kneeling now, and seeming to struggle with a man all in red. He started to run forward, the smell of weed and mud was horrible; he fell and slid on the mud, and the whipping water flew in his face like cat's spite. The man in red, he was half out of the water now and crying; Liam could hear him shrieking as though the wind was in his voice. Liam was on the causeway now, on his hands and knees for safety; his cap had gone and the water broke over him and ran down his jersey neck and blinded him. He saw with appalling clarity the man in red and Jamie Murphy fall together into the river, struggling, and he could not tell from the strangling water whether it was their heads or wave crests which showed for a moment, or whether it was they who cried aloud or the howling wind.

He crawled back finally, stricken. He clutched the grass on the bank and wept and retched. Old Barlow had told the tale of the Red Man of the Boyne who waits for men to drown and cries in triumph, and he had seen him, seen him with his own eyes, and heard his voice which was more a voice of winds.

There was mourning too in the tinker camp the next day; young Stimon on his way back from town had taken the causeway as usual, poor foolish boy on a night like that. His father, on the opposite bank, worried at his lateness and, fearing that he might still take the river way home, had seen him dimly in the far lights, seen him taken by a gust and fall and be washed away. And the other man, God rest his soul, had run on to the causeway and tried to pull him from the rage of the waters. Stimon could not swim; he had panicked, pulling Jamie Murphy with him, but of this the old man knew nothing. No one knew. Only that both had gone, and Stimon wearing the new red jersey his mam had given him the day before. . . .

'LIM A SHROYNYA THOMAN NEEDIAS MISLI RILHU. GOSHTA RILHU NEEDIAS, GART LAKINS AND GART SWIBLIS, STAYSH AND KRISH GLOCHI AND KRISH KARBS MUKINYA LIM A SHROYNYA. LASHULEST NEEDHAS YOU COULD MISLI, SKAI AND SLOOFA AND KEN THOMS . . . STAYSH GRADIS NEEDIAS RILHU. . . .'

'By the banks of the Boyne many people go mad. Numbers of mad people, young girls and boys, yes and old men and women too, dwell near the Boyne. It's the loveliest place where you could walk, with water and wood and houses of great folks . . . but it drives people mad. . . .'

So went the say of old John Barlow, spoken in his own tongue, in the language of Shelta, the old man of the wagon-dwellers, camped by the riverside these last weeks.

Spare him a word, a smile. It is little. He will look up, and answer you: 'Good luck, sir. And blessings on you. . . .'

The Return of Sagittarius

NO STONE remains one upon the other this day of Jenny Malone's house. There is a desolation of briar and thorn where once her small garden coloured the bare hillside; yet I can remember when it glowed like a piece of my mother's patchwork from among the browns and grey-greens that were the colours of the old hill.

The pipit and the raven have made their homes there now, and the high hill rears dark and desolate, and deep in its heart dwells an unquiet spirit. We will tell you of the strange things that happened on the dark hill, we, the old men. Of the lost unhappy thing that cries on nights of storm when blackness binds the head of the hill and thunder tears the womb of heaven. Then we shut out the night from our houses, we, the old men, and the valley crouches and turns away from the lonely hill and its terrible neighing cry of despair.

It began long years ago when our fathers were at the fine beginning of their lives, that young Jenny Malone left the village and went away to the great hill to live with her uncle. Jenny's parents died young, and she had been reared by kind-hearted neighbours as one of their own large family and swallowed into their lives almost unnoticed. One more mouth hardly mattered. But she was a silent and secretive child who preferred to play alone in the fields, and who found the noise and bustle of her companions too much for her quiet nature. In their turn they thought her odd; mooning about all day doing nothing; no good at school because she stared out of the window into the sunlight and watched only the clouds pass by the trees, and the birds on the branches. No good teasing her because she didn't go red and screech or fly at you; she just walked away with her head high like a queen. But they'd been told to be kind to her as she had no father or mother to herself; if they weren't they got a good lamming, so it was best to leave her alone and let her do what she pleased. She didn't get in the way of their games, so what did it matter; she only wanted to be by herself, and she was the only one brave enough to climb to the very top of the great hill, and on the way down to stay a little time with her old uncle in the small stone house. This was more than any of them dared to do; they feared the great rocks that crouched like beasts on the hill, the cries of the death-black ravens, and most of all they feared Jenny's uncle, who talked and laughed a lot to himself, and had a long white beard and leant always on a black crooked stick.

When Jenny was nearly sixteen it was decided she should go and live with the old man, who was her only relation, and who badly needed someone to look after him, lonely on the hillside.

And Jenny was pleased to go. She had been happy enough with the good neighbours who had reared her, but glad to be going at last to one of her kin, and anxious in her young way to look after the old man who was the only link with her own blood. So Jenny went away up the hillside to the small stone house which seemed only a white speck seen from the village below.

She tended the garden and kept the small house tidy and clean while the old man chuckled in the sun with the wind pulling at his long hair, watching with faded eyes the bright flowers she had grown so carefully—wrestling with the greedy bracken that threatened to strangle the little garden, and building up the wall all round with stones from the hillside to keep away the biting winds in winter.

Thus the last years drifted by the old man's singing head, he became filled with dreams and was shaken often by small laughter; for the years went by like thistledown and his heart was warmed by the bright flowers and he smiled and dreamed and dreamed and slept.

Death came to him very early on a morning of white mist, and drew the old man, unreluctant, to the green churchyard below the great hill where the elm trees slept a rook-filled sleep, and the biting winds held no more crying.

A stone was taken from the hillside, and Jenny left with him some of the bright flowers he loved from the little garden.

All the stones in the green churchyard had come from the great hill; crouching, lurching, snarling grey on the hillside, the untamed stones watched over the little churchyard and the village, all made from the body of the old hill; stones from the hillside smoothed and tamed by the hands of men.

Jenny returned up the hill alone. There were many among the young men of the village who would have taken her to wife, but she was deer-shy, and her eyes were restless as a March sky. They courted her, my father among them, but her laughter held the wildness of curlew cry and the great hill was no place for lovers. So the young men went their ways and took the girls of the valley for wives, and the warm darkness of the lanes and hedgerows welcomed their love.

Jenny was not seen for months at a time, and the villagers, at first curious, grew unheeding and in time forgetful.

No creature gave Jenny companionship; no dog or cat sat by her fire. Silent and secret she had always been, but now she was like the foxes on the hillside, the stone house a refuge only as the hole in the rock is the home of the hill fox. And the year rolled round the head of the old hill.

One night, when summer lay warm over the land as a hen bird on her nest, the moon shone like a crown over the hill. The whispering and stirring of the night rose into strange music to Jenny, and the scent of the earth was like wine. As though a harp was hidden in its heart, the old hill was humming under the stars, and all the planets sang. She felt her heart beating with the black heart of the old hill, and her blood running dark like the river. She saw the moon chained motionless to the earth, and the earth held in a trance by the power of the moon, and over the hill came the thunder.

She grew afraid as the sound became greater; for it was not of the heavens, of the black storm-clouds and cracking whip of lightning, but thunder rolling and wracking from the earth.

She ran from the door and crouched under the ash tree which grew out from the rocks behind the house. The earth seemed to roll beneath her, and she saw a great black horse, black as the rivers of hell, who came up the hill like the north wind flying, and the thunder of the earth lay in his hooves. She ran from the ash tree to see him pass, but he saw her movement and shuddered to a stand, wheeling to meet the scent of her, his mane entangled in the stars and his tail falling like water.

Silence crept back over the hill to where Jenny and the stallion stood looking at one another under the moon. The blackness of his great body filled the night; powerful and nervous he watched her. His gaze burst upon her; she could see the moons blazing in his eyes, and she went slowly, as in a dream, to his side. Above her he towered, his head holding the burning planets like a banner.

She touched the black rainbow of his neck and he breathed into her face with sweetness. Wondering, she moved closer, to the great chest whose strength could turn aside the whirlwind, and his mane fell over her shoulders, heavy with her own hair. Jenny never saw him again, but after that night Crazy Jenny kept the light of the moon in her eye. The years passed and Crazy Jenny laughed and grew old, and we in the valley grew out of our childhood and took upon us the cares of men. Our fathers one by one were taken to the green churchyard, and each beneath a tall grey stone from the old hill.

And at last old Crazy Jenny was carried down the steep track away from the stone house, away from the old hill, to rest beside our fathers, so many of whom had offered her their hearts as fine young men. But now all lay cold together, and only the stones from the hillside were left to tell one from another. Nothing of value was left in Jenny's house; we climbed the hill to look, but only the everyday things of her use were there, and in one corner, sheeted in cobwebs, an old-fashioned cradle. Poor Jenny, we said, crazy for years and all alone with no child to comfort her woman's heart at the end. Perhaps she had pretended a baby had lain there, and on winter nights perhaps she had rocked it and sung over it to take away the crying from the wind. The small house soon fell into a ruin, the stones crumbling in one upon the other. It became a home for the white ghost-owl, and the garden vanished under the strong green fingers of the hill. *But something had been left upon the hill, something that cried on the storm-winds, the last secret of Crazy Jenny. . . .*

It was on a night of rain and high winds shortly after her death that we heard the first sounds of frenzied galloping and a voice crying from the great hill. But we slept heavily in the village, and were not aroused until too late. Only the tinkers camping outside the village heard the squire's blood mare hurl herself at the field gate and gallop away up the hill after the sound of the flying hooves.

And on every night of storm, under cover of the howling wind, a horse would break out of stable or field and gallop madly away into the roaring night.

We thought it the work of a horse thief, making his raids perhaps from the cover of the hill; someone who knew our fear of it, and our reluctance to set foot there . . . and the young Sara said she'd seen him; on a night when there was no wind, only the low clouds racing over the face of the hill, silently, forerunners of the gale to come. He was standing on the path outside the churchyard, but the night being dark she hadn't seen well. She had touched the horse's body, and it had seemed to her hand—a horse-knowing hand—black, powerful, yet strangely gentle. A horse of blood. Of

the man she saw little, save that he seemed tall, and part of the horse. She had felt no fear of horse or man. But we took her tale with laughter, for Sara was light in her head, and with a tinker girl you never knew that she mightn't be playing at some game of half belief with herself, as well as anyone who'd care to listen. So we laughed at yellow-haired Sara with her shifting eyes blue as the jay's wing, and her vixen's face with the thoughts passing like cloud shadow. The winds came the next day, as the running clouds had foretold, and in the night the tinkers' horses broke away. The sound of hooves roared in the little camp, and in the confusion of fallen tents and the crying of the women no one noticed Sara had gone. We had already decided to band together and search for the lost horses and bring down the horse thief to justice, but before the light had come to the morning Dearg Peadar from the camp ran to us crying that Sara was gone.

We feared now that the man might have taken her; perhaps he meant it only in joking to show what a fine fellow he was, or perhaps Sara had run after the horses and stayed with them all night on the hillside. Perhaps . . . Dearg Peadar's face twisted like a fox with the hounds on him . . . *God help him if he has done harm to her. . . .*

The tinker men came with us, and we fanned out over the hillside and began to climb with the first grey light from the east. O'Hanrahan and I had our guns, for the man might show violence, and he might now be more than just a horse thief. Peadar saw him first with his tinker's eye quick as a hawk's; leaning on a rock and looking down upon the village lights below, and all around him a herd of horses grazing, the squire's blood mare delicate among them. He hadn't seen us, so intently was he watching, and the wind took away the scent of us from the horses.

Of Sara we could see no sign.

O'Hanrahan decided to fire a shot over his head and frighten him into coming with us without fighting, even if it should mean stampeding the horses. But perhaps it was the uncertain light, the way it is at dawn, or perhaps the man moved, for with the shot we saw him fling up his arms and fall from sight behind the rock. As we ran forward there was a great rush of horses down the hill towards the village, and Sara started up from the heather in front of them before we could shout a warning to her. We saw the yellow hair fall under the sea of horses rolling down the hillside, and Peadar turned from us and ran yelping like a hurt dog to where she lay. Poor broken Sara; her head would hold no fancies now. The others went back to Peadar's side, but O'Hanrahan and I climbed up to the rock and there lay the terrible body of the poor creature we had hunted, for you couldn't call him a man, this last secret held by Crazy Jenny.

His arms were stretched out, his hands had pulled up the heather in his last despair, and the great body that was yet part of him was still twitching, black as night with folded forelegs and mighty hooves, and the great fine tail spread out like a shroud

y. . . .

We saw his face was gentle as we turned it from the heather, but even death had not taken away the torment from it. We saw now why he had taken Sara—young Sara who had felt his gentleness in the dark, and had no fear. He had called to the horses from the night, and he had longed so greatly for the companionship no horse could give, yet knowing the horror his appearance would inspire.

And he had no way of telling of his need and longing, for his voice was the voice of a horse. We buried the poor creature where he lay, and piled upon him a great mound of grey stones from the hill, that nothing should disturb his secret. And we came down from the hill young no longer. No horse would approach the old hill then, and none will this day; and it is many long years ago since we carried Sara of the yellow hair down to the valley where her people lamented with the sound of hound-voices, a savage baying sound that darkened our hearts.

We, the old men, will soon be gone, and the strange story of the old hill will be forgotten; one by one we leave our friends and go to join our fathers in the green churchyard, and our children, not knowing what we know, will only hear the crying of the wind.

The few of us who remain still fear the nights of storm; as long as we remain alive there is no forgetting, and when the rain flings upon the old hill and all the winds of heaven howl, we shut out the night from our houses and talk a little louder, each afraid of the black winds and with the sting of pity in his heart. We pray for the kind light of morning when a silence will fall over the old hill, and the little song of pipits ripple down the hillside. The larks will rise to sing away the fears of the night, and we the grey old men praise the sweet larks, for it is only with birdsong that the great hill can forget the desolation of the winds and its dreams.

A Breeder of Connemaras

MY BROTHER told me this; here in the County Meath it is hard to believe, for here is peace and the green grazing lands; a county of fine horses and bullocks which grow as fast as do mushrooms in the night, and slow sheep that fatten carefully as though clipped into their sheep shapes from the start. But go west and west again to where the sea bites out the land and spits the fragments into all the little bays; and slides and separates headlands from islands, and cold fingers the feet of mountains far inland. To Connemara, near to the place where men take green stones from a mountain, so laced with the sea's design and green as deep water you would think the sea froze there turning time into stone. Where cloud and sea join and you cannot see the birth of one nor the death of the other, nor where the sea has her mountains and the land her waters. Land means much here, more than we could know. Even the bitter brown lands, the black bogs, the dark heather and the brushed thorn; lands walled with stone and growing only stone, and where green is startling as danger. Ravens and curlews are there, and the wild geese. And the wildest of the white swans. Yet brother covets brother's croft, so beautiful the land takes the heart from you, so bitter it turns men as grey as the mountain ewes in their hopeless attendance on its harsh reign.

This land is a barbarous queen; she will kill and twist her court, her supplicants, as easily as she will smile with such sweetness that men would die enchanted, swearing they heard the bells of Heaven, when only a lark is rising.

Well, you can cut a little hay here, turn over fair potatoes; a pig will keep itself, if not fat then reasonable; goats thrive anywhere where men fail and seem to take a delight in it, devil's horns and all, and the small grey sheep are everywhere all on the mountain; some bullocks, though not many, and here and there the yellow ponies of Connemara.

The Joyce brothers had one side of a mountain each. Neither side was favoured, except Conn had the sun a little more on it and a better cottage, and he was a breeder of Connemaras.

Not in a big way, as some do around Clifden, with the luck of money behind them, and the blessings of good land, but he kept the old sort with the yellow coats to them, some as bright as buttercups and others pale like reeds on a lake, and all with black legs. They had fine long hooked heads; Spanish, Conn thought them, and though he kept a few greys and blacks, most were the dun colour, for he had no favour for any of the fashionable colours such as the white-maned ones which won at the shows. Conn was very sure these were not strong, however pretty they looked, and he kept his strain hard with the use of only the yellow stallions with the dark legs and the line down the back.

For the other Joyce had only some few sheep on his side of the mountain, and if there was rain, which God knows was often enough, then it fell on his side, or so he had it, in a very bitter manner indeed. And very often it did seem this way, for where Donal's side was black under cloud, Conn's would be under a shaft of sun as bright as the flash on a jay's wing.

In short, everything was against Donal, and he would have done anything to get Conn's side of the mountain for his too. The only thing was, he had no love for the little horses, as had Conn. They were as different as brothers could possibly be. And every time Conn's yellow stallion crossed on to Donal's grounds then it was a mercy it returned, for poison and shotguns filled the poor man's mind whenever he saw the clatter of sods—thrown up by not just one, but where the stallion went there went all the mares

and colts too, across everything.

Donal's sheep picked over Conn's side too, and his bullocks were always to be found there when he wanted them, but Conn wasn't worried and that annoyed Donal even more, as he had no case for complaint whatsoever. Neither brother had taken matrimony into view. Conn had his horses, which, wild as they were, were to him more amenable than any woman, and when he had hold of one, at least it couldn't loose its tongue at him. Conn hated talk, specially women's; his mother had nagged his father into an early grave, and nagged most of his brothers away to America (where they still heard her), and they say you can talk the hind leg off a donkey—well, even the ass left home after that and went right away nearly to Limerick so as to avoid such a fate. All Ma Joyce was left with in the end—and she didn't die till ninety-eight, and that almost absent-mindedly—was an old dog, mercifully deaf, and a clatter of Leghorns which had plenty to say themselves. Donal was too bitter for any woman to consider. One squeeze and you'd most likely get a pip in the eye. My brother was down that way for ponies, which was how he heard it all.

There was a sharp corner to the road right opposite Donal's cottage which took many by surprise; perhaps it was because the wall round his lower field was of green stones; it deceived the eye. Anyway, like others before him, he went into it and there he was, stranded miles from any place. Half of it was speed, for my brother is a desperate driver, but half was the yellow stallion he saw in the field and which pulled him up short. It was the finest Connemara he'd seen in years—he'd even have said the best. The big concrete gateposts to the field were broken down and an iron bed filled the gap. The cottage near by was empty and nearly in ruins.

The same corner had earlier confounded the bishop on his annual diocesan round. The village still talked of it. The august figure had surveyed the frayed wheel, the forlorn country, the rain, his minions whose duties had not included tyre repairs in their curriculum, the road going on for mile on mile, and one transfixed sheep which stared back at the bishop in wonderment and forgot even to chew.

All waited for the pronouncement—the Spirit triumphing over the discomforts of mortal flesh.

'We'll foot it,' said His Grace; and walked the six miles to the village, as my brother had to himself. There, later on, inquiring about whose was the yellow stallion, he was told of the trick played by that same bend in the road on the Joyce brothers, Conn and Donal.

Well, as I said, Conn went to America. Suddenly he left everything, ponies and all. Donal waited and waited on, but heard no more from him. In the course of things, Donal took on Conn's side of the mountain, and one of the first things he did was to get in all Conn's ponies and sell them off. All except the yellow stallion, who became the bane of his life, trampling over everything Donal planted, neighing under his window at night, chasing his ewes about like a mad collie, and generally annoying the heart and soul out of him. In the end Donal decided to shoot him. Meanwhile, he had tidied up his place considerably and even gone to the trouble of putting up a powerful pair of concrete gateposts to his lower field, where the path off the road went over it and up to his croft a half-mile or so up under the mountain. People said it looked like the entrance now to one of the grand houses of the country.

The stallion was the cause of the whole thing, if you looked at it like that.

McCulloch's lorry, which young Dennis drove like a Jehu as usual, and with a ton of sheep up for market, didn't it overturn just on that corner, sheep and young Dennis all together in the wreckage? Yet not one hurt, the stallion belting back up the road as fast as he'd come down it, which was why young Dennis had braked too hard anyway and the concrete posts shattered like eggshells.

And wasn't Conn Joyce there, for all to see, grinning and stiff as a sentry in a box, where Donal had mixed him into the concrete and set him up as neat as you please into the left-hand gatepost. Hardly changed at all. Not even his red hair. He was chipped out and given a decent burial, you will be glad to hear, for they are a very religious family, the Joyces. And although Conn was always said by the women to have a heart of stone, you could hardly expect it to be so true, could you now?

The Kerry Bull

Now when Sean Murphy's old black bull died, no one was really surprised. That is to say, a death is always something of a surprise, and in the case of the old bull expected for a long time, but when death came up with him on the hill above Inchoney it made a marvellous, disquieting sight out of the old one. In life he was as big as a church tower, with horns that grew not in the stabbing manner of the Kerry at all, but outward and up with a flourish to the narrow ends neat enough to hook a hazel off a twig with no bother at all.

And to see him come up out of the bog on a morning of mist was something to put the heart across you, for he was a regular old Time of a bull as his great head scythed the morning into two parts, and if you were a child you moved in mortal fear to hear his big twisted feet clackering after you.

Tommy once read in a book where the hero was caught looking into a Turkish harem, where all the naked women were, and a big black guard came slap-thucking up the marble passages after him, scimitar whirling and a bull's roar from the heart, something like Murphy's old one there on the hill.

And now he was dead, a green foam coming out from between his long piano teeth as though he'd coughed up the Atlantic, and he'd spoilt one of his great horns which had broken as he fell on it sideways, and his black belly piled up as big as a coal bunker, and how we children exclaimed at his eyes, which were gone back into his head and dull with a blue fly's sheen to them. Once they used to burn you up like the sun when it strikes brown loch water,

now they were jelly under your finger. A grey hair, as curly as in a water-dog's coat, was in his forehead's curls, somehow very unexpected and sad.

For none of us knew that his heart was gentle all these years, and the lorry men who came and pulled him down on to the road with a horse didn't know either, and because he'd been seen that morning climbing on to the skinny ridge-back of Ma Sheahy's spotted heifer they laughed and called him game to the end.

Well, anyway, he was dead, and all the people in the valley and above on the hill wondered where they would be taking their cows now, or whether at last they'd have to get in the insemination lads with their little grey van and their mysterious paraphernalia.

We kids were always highly intrigued by them, and knew a farmer up in the next village had a crop of white-faced, lovely calves from the rubber funnels or whatever it was they shoved up the poor mother cows, and all the talk was of Herefords and Angus. No raggy-tempered Kerry was ever used though, as their owners proudly said a Kerry bull was too clever by half to be kidded into such a performance, and a Kerry cow would as like turn on the brave lads and use her horn on them in the very place they thought they were about to fiddle with; I'm telling you. However, all were safe in calf or milk, so there was no urgency to the matter at all for a while yet, and maybe Sean Murphy would be getting another bull, for he was a decent man and very obliging to his neighbours.

And possibly not even a whippy young Kerry at that, but a white polly Hereford which counts at market. A soft, amiable beast no doubt, and free of the troublesome nature of the Kerry—but would he go down for a bite on the seashore in the hard weather do you suppose, as do the brave Kerries when feed is bare on the mountains?

So you can see the whole question about bulls is of some importance in these parts, or I would not be on about the creatures at such length.

And the death of such a one as Sean Murphy's leaves a space as it were in the community such as ours, both in the human and particularly among the bereaved cows. And with such a character as the old one, well, it is like losing one of the family, and God save the thought of that . . .

And now I come to the other one in this story, because although the Kerry bulls are the meat of it and it must be established firmly in the mind that the Kerries are everything in these parts, the real one that matters used to live over the far side of the bay, close to a strand which you could swear was made of white pearls, the shine was so white and strong from it in a certain light.

Roisin O'Meara and her pa lived there, in one of the last of the older cabins, still thatched but as whiskery as a Donegal goat from neglect. At certain times we all repaired there when the story-teller came round, for this was traditional still with us. Padraic O'Shea was the man's name, and he knew of things too far beyond this little land, and his stories were wonderful to all of us, young and old. Sure the films was with us as well, but no nearer than Ballybeg, and that fifteen miles to the north of us.

It was known to us and for many years that, even as the tiny child, Roisin and her pa Seamus were not well together; Seamus was a hard man all round, hard with his friends, with his money, with his fists and with his daughter too, for he had very little use for women. His wife, poor soul, died quite young after a life few women could have stood, and made worse by the loneliness. For should a man have few friends, then few will visit him and his family, even should they live in the heart of a great city. Far out on the strand of Killaloe, with a journey across bog and stream, and a mile on still with only the black mountain at the cabin's back, even St Patrick might be forgiven the journey. . . .

And indeed he might have done at that, for the soul of Seamus O'Meara was a dark one, we were believing, and a triumph for any saint to win for the Faith.

Now Roisin had beauty—the true beauty which now and again is seen in these parts and which some say comes from the Galway-Spanish—but she could not come to school like all of us because she was so often ill. It seemed that, as well as a general kind of illness which came and went, she was also lame, but strangely that too came and went, for some days she would be as blithe as a blackbird and could even run on the shore of the strand like any of us, but others she could only drag her foot with difficulty and her face was shut tight. Yet she could swim like a herring without hindrance or fear, though never if she thought herself watched.

As she grew older neither condition improved, and, although many a man would have given her his heart, some were feared that all was not well with her mind. There was talk once of Seamus and a woman from Cork getting wed, but it was only talk,

for Roisin at the time became suddenly ill and could not walk for weeks. Seamus had to put off his wedding there for good, although I doubt if the woman would have taken him on if she'd seen where she had to live after the city life, or Roisin with her fits of crying.

The following winter was hard, with snow, and the little Kerry cows, as they have always done, picked at the cold sea's edge for the stray weed thrown up by the gales. Padraic was at the O'Mearas twice, as was his custom no matter what the weather told, and at the second time he spoke of beasts and fishes and tales of other lands as well as of our own known stories, for he knew them all. Some were marvellously like our own tales of times long gone, but the day I mind he told of the white bull who carried the young girl across the sea on his back, and being cattle-minded we listened knowingly to his description of the beast, which, except for its milky coat, was apparently much like Sean's great old black. And Padraic spoke of its big dark eyes and the curls round its horns and how quietly it let itself be led around by the girl and her companions, who made wreaths for its neck, and smoothed its silky dewlap which fell like a white sheet to its knees.

The rest of the story was not Christian at all and somewhat hard to believe, but we remembered every word said on the bull, and Roisin was in the corner of the fireplace with her face alight from the flames, and nodding excitedly as though she knew what that young lass in the tale felt when she saw such a beast as that. But then Roisin had never felt the fear we had for the old black one, which used to make us feel bad, as she had no way to run as we could, should he ever make after her.

Well, winter left us at last and with the spring of the year Sean had it that he must get himself another bull of one sort or another, as the cows must be put into calf again without delay, and too much delay in the matter already. On Saturday he put the cob to, and left for the Tullyane sales, taking with him Seamus and some others for counsel and company. There must be no rash judgment this day.

And what happened when they had gone was in its own way a miracle, though hardly one Father Malley could have hoped for, it not being of the Faith at all.

And true, it was no great white bull that was the cause of it, but a little snidey Kerry from over the far side of the strand. The explanation was there, right in Seamus's own herd of cows, and the wind bearing their scent across the water to where yon black one would have been picking over the seaweed on the sea's edge. He never walked a step of the way, but didn't he take to the water and swim the five miles to come down with the tide at last towards Seamus's lands.

Roisin told it afterwards that she was taking the first swim that year when all she saw was the black head of a bull a-shoving through the water till he was nearly atop of her, and then she got such a clipe from one of his legs that she went under. To save herself she caught at anything she could, which happened to be the bull, and fought to surface, which no doubt frightened the little bull so that both of them found themselves out on the running tide and unable to make any but the stretch of strand where the Lynches had their boats and croft, some three miles to the west.

Young Danny Lynch was patching a boat when he saw, with disbelief at first, a black bull and a girl half over its shoulder pushing in to the strand almost to where he stood. The bull found foot first and the girl fell crying out back into the water as he humped out on to land and shook himself like a dog. But Danny got to her in no time and got her up to the house, where, from the moment she left the water, Roisin walked as firm and upright as a young stag. Well, as Granny Lynch said, it couldn't happen to a bishop.

And there's an end to this tale. Danny and Roisin were married and live on the Lynch croft only a hen's race away from where it all happened; where Roisin rode in from the sea on the back of a bull just as in Padraic's tale, though not so flowery, and Danny was mending his pa's boat.

She has never had a day's sickness from then till now, and walked later to Seamus's burial, there and back without thought. The bull the Lynches kept, for they thought him lucky, and no one came for his return. His calves carry a mark on their foreheads which some think spoil them, and call him no true Kerry to throw such a mark, which is in the shape of a half-moon. But again the Lynches think him lucky, and he is now a big one, though kind for a Kerry.

Roisin puts it all down to him; perhaps it was the kick that did it, or the shock that unlocked the door, so to speak, as Padraic said.

It would seem that Padraic knows, for he was not amazed at all.